TROPHY WIFE

The Jilted Wives Club, Book 2

BETHANY LOPEZ

Trophy Wife
Copyright 2021 Bethany Lopez
Published August 2021
ISBN - 978-1-954655-05-8

Cover Design by Allison Martin
Editing by Red Road Editing / Kristina Circelli
Ebook Formatting by Bethany Lopez

Want to learn more about my books? Sign up for my newsletter and Join my FB Group/Street Team!
http://crea.tf/bethanylopeznewsletter
https://www.facebook.com/groups/1443318612574585/

Created with Vellum

For my children... always strive to be better, stay strong, and love with all your heart!

1
SUMMER

I made my way down the city street, practically skipping as I hurried to meet my favorite people in the world for dinner ... The *Jilted Wives Club*.

The club only consisted of me and my friends, Whitney and Margo, but still, it was the best club ever.

We'd met a year ago when we'd all tried, and failed, to attend a support group for women who'd recently divorced from their cheating bastard exes. Well, at least in all three of our cases, that was accurate. I wasn't sure about the other women, since I'd only made it through one tearful exchange before I'd bolted from the room.

Since then, Whitney had met and fallen in love with Luca, this completely wonderful and sweet *younger* man who truly was the yin to her yang.

I wanted to find a yin, but so far, I'd been unlucky.

You know how they say you have to kiss a lot of frogs to find your prince? Well, let's just say I'm covered in metaphorical warts from head to toe and so far ... no prince.

I'd gone on blind dates, set up by Whitney, tried meeting guys in bars with Margo, and had been sporadically using a dating app for more than six months, but kept coming up empty.

I mean, not all the guys were bad...

A few of them had been really nice, but there'd been no spark.

A couple had sparks for days but were jerks.

Then there were the weirdos. The one who asked if he could rub my feet ... on our first date ... at the table ... in a restaurant. Then the guy whose profile picture was of a looped belt and some lube.

Suffice it to say, finding Mr. Right wasn't easy, but I wasn't giving up.

Sure, my first husband had been married when he started dating me, without my knowledge of course. By the time I'd found out, I'd been completely in love, and he'd vowed to leave his wife. I'd only been in my early twenties when we'd gotten married, and he'd been much older, officially making me his *trophy wife*. Although I naively thought we'd be together forever, he'd done the same thing to me that he'd done to his first wife.

Cheated. But this time with a woman older than me who oddly resembled his first wife. He eventually left me for her.

I don't know why I thought Jared would be different with me. Once a cheater, always a cheater, right?

Margo would say it's because I trust too easily. And she'd be right.

A deep voice catcalled as I neared the restaurant and I turned to see a group of men working at a construction site across the street.

I lifted my hand to wave and yelled back, "*Thanks*," before opening the door and walking inside.

As my eyes adjusted to the change in light, Whit caught my attention by raising her hand to let me know where they were seated.

"I see my friends," I told the hostess before she could ask me how many were in my party and moved through the dining room to the back, where my friends were waiting. "Hi!"

"Hey, girl," Whit said as she got out of her chair to give me a hug. "Margo's on with a client."

I looked over at Margo, who winked at me but continued her conversation, and took one of the empty seats.

"I'm so happy it's Thursday," I said as I picked up the menu.

We met every Thursday for dinner, unless something important came up, but so far at least two of us had been able to make it every week. We took turns choosing the restaurant and were yet to go back to any place twice.

It was fun and exciting, kind of a dining adventure, and I looked forward to the next Thursday as soon as I woke up on Friday.

Today we were trying a new Peruvian place.

"How's your week been?" I asked Whitney, lowering my voice so as not to disrupt Margo's call.

"Good," she said, taking a sip of wine. "Silas's lacrosse team had a tournament last weekend, so we pretty much spent all of our time there, but it was fun. You should have heard Luca screaming his head off like a soccer mom. It was great."

"Sorry," Margo said as she disconnected her call. "What'd I miss?"

"Nothing yet," I said, barely able to contain my excitement. "I almost couldn't wait to show you guys ... This guy popped up on my *'for you'* page of the app and I've been dying to talk to you about him."

"Someone you're interested in?" Whit asked.

"Yeah," I said, pulling out my phone and bringing up the app. "I haven't touched the app since he popped up. I didn't want to click yes on his profile until I showed him to you and got your opinion. Plus, I guess I'm a little nervous. I mean, what if I like his profile and then he doesn't like mine back?"

"Let's see," Margo said, holding out her hand.

"Okay, but don't press anything," I warned as I handed her the phone with the profile opened.

"Noah," Margo read aloud. "He's cute, in a bookish, professorish kind of way."

"*He is*," I nearly squealed. "He's a professor and it says he loves books."

"It does ... and he loves dogs, sitting in the rain, and playing *Words with Friends*."

"*This* guy is your type?" Whitney asked, looking a little baffled.

I knew people looked at me, a petite blonde with big boobs and a small waist, and figured I'd be a gold digger who went after older men with sports cars and AmEx black cards, but Whitney wasn't trying to put me in a box like that. She'd asked me a few months ago to tell her my type so she could set me up, and Noah was the opposite of what I'd told her.

But that's only because guys like Noah never went for me and I'd been afraid to ask for something I couldn't have. But now he was right there on my phone, and I wanted more than anything to press *yes*.

"Oh, yes, he is ... just look at him. With that floppy brown hair and those adorable glasses. Don't you just want to eat him up?"

"I wouldn't kick him out of bed," Margo said, passing me the phone back right as I reached for it.

When I grabbed it, my thumb accidentally pressed the *no* button, and his picture disappeared.

"*Nooooo*," I cried, trying unsuccessfully to swipe him back into existence.

"What happened?" Whitney asked.

"He's gone."

"Can't you get him back? Search up his name or something?" Margo asked.

"No, there are no last names shown, and you can't search by name. I pressed no, so I don't know if he'll ever pop up in my algorithm again," I explained, looking at my phone sadly. "He's gone."

2

NOAH

A knock on my office door had me letting out a frustrated sigh before calling, "Come in."

I looked absently at my watch, noting I still had five minutes of office hours left, and glanced up from the papers I'd been grading to see one of my students from my *Literary Dimensions on Film* course. It was one of the easier classes I taught and one I usually found entertaining.

Unfortunately, most students took it thinking it would give them an easy A, and it was usually about now, mid-semester, when they started popping in during my office hours, either hoping to drop the class or find some way to bring their grade up.

"It's Ms. Sinclair, correct?" I asked, not bothering to get up since she'd walked in and flopped down into the chair across from me.

She nodded rapidly, causing her long dark hair to cover her face briefly before she pushed it back and bit her lower lip.

"What can I do for you?" I asked, when rather than reply she just stared at me with wide eyes and her lower lip still grasped between her teeth.

I wondered if it hurt, gnawing on her lip that way, but rather than ask, I simply waited for her to respond to one or both of my questions.

After a few more seconds of not blinking or letting her poor lip free, she rolled her eyes and sat up in the chair. As she perched herself on the edge and arched her back, Ms. Sinclair seemed to watch me for a reaction.

Which was concerning since I was the one waiting to see why she'd come to see me.

Maybe she had a speech impediment...

"Ms. Sinclair?" I prodded, as I watched the big hand on my wall clock move, indicating my office hours were over. "Is there something you wanted to see me about?"

Her whole body seemed to deflate, and she muttered something under her breath that sounded oddly like, "*Clueless*," and I couldn't help but wonder if she was talking about me, or herself.

"My paper on *Little Women*," she began.

Thrilled she was finally getting to the point, I leaned forward on my desk and laced my fingers together.

"Comparing the book to the twenty-nineteen film," I filled in, hoping to help her get to the point.

"Yes. You gave me a C."

I nodded because it was true. "And?"

"Why?" she asked, letting out a sharp breath. "It was a good paper."

"I could tell from reading that you watched the film," I told her. "But did you actually read the book?"

She gave a half shrug and said, "Most of it."

"And that's why you received a C," I informed her. "If you had read the book and then watched the most recent adaptation, you would have written about the many changes the screenwriter made and given your opinion on said changes. Instead, you gave me a movie review, which, although entertaining, missed the mark of the assignment."

"Is there anything I can do to bring up the grade?" she asked, her voice sounding oddly nasally all of a sudden.

"You can read the book in its entirety and this time write a paper actually comparing the book to the recent film. The highest grade you'd be able to get would be a B, since it would be turned in late, but that's better than a C."

Ms. Sinclair scowled and stood up. She glanced at me briefly, before turning and dropping her things to the floor. She bent over at the waist to pick them up, and when she glanced at me over her shoulder, I asked, "Do you need help?" But all she did was scowl more darkly, grab her things, and flee the room.

I shook my head as I wondered why my students seemed to get stranger with each passing year, then I shoved my laptop and the papers I still needed to grade into my briefcase, before exiting my office, locking it behind me.

"Noah."

I stopped and turned to see Trent, one of my colleagues and good friends, coming down the hall toward me.

"Hey," I said as he reached me. "How was your day?"

"Another great day in the lab," he replied. Trent was a biology professor. "Was that another nubile young student in need of help I saw exiting your office?"

I gave him a dry look and shook my head. "Just a student looking to improve her grade."

"I bet," Trent joked. He liked to mess with me when it came to my female, and some male, students. I figured it was because he was married and knew I was perpetually single. "Must be nice, being the sexy professor they all daydream about."

"Give me a break," I countered. "I'm practically old enough to be their father, or at least older uncle. There's no way these twenty-something kids are attracted to me."

"Right," he said dryly. "Because young girls with daddy issues would never fantasize about their smart, slightly dorky professor, who is completely oblivious when it comes to his effect on the opposite sex."

"Are you done?" I asked, tired of reliving this conversation on what felt like a daily basis. "Are you headed straight home, or do you have time for a drink?"

"Cam and Tucker are having dinner with her mom, so I'm free to join you at the bar. Maybe we can hook you up with a woman your own age," he added with a grin.

"A beer and some wings will suit me just fine," I told him as we walked out of the building.

"If you say so," Trent said, still grinning. "But I can't wait until you finally meet a woman who drives you so crazy you forget all these stuffy rules you have for yourself."

I just shook my head and moved toward my car.

It hadn't happened yet, and I was beginning to think it never would.

3

SUMMER

"Hey, Mom, I only have a few minutes left on my break, but wanted to check up on you," I said, holding my phone in place with my shoulder as I opened my glass water bottle. "How are you feeling?"

"Better," she said, although her voice still sounded weak to my ears.

My mother had been sick off and on for the last few months. I kept begging her to go to the doctor and get checked out, but she was stubborn and had a deep-rooted fear of hospitals.

"Have you been getting enough rest?"

"I'm fine, Summer," my mother insisted. She'd raised me on her own since I was four, although half the time it felt like I was the one raising her. "I even took a walk to the park this morning."

"Oh, well, I'm sure the fresh air was good for you, but don't push it, okay?" I asked, worried she was doing just that.

I made a mental note to go by her house after work with some soup, then pulled my phone away from my ear to check the time.

"I've got to get back to work," I told her once I saw my break was almost over. "Helen has to leave early today."

Helen was my mom's best friend and had been like a second mother to me. She owned a boutique clothing store, and I was her manager and occasional buyer.

"Tell her she owes me ten bucks. Oh, I almost forgot to tell you what Cassandra told me at the park ... Jared's having a baby."

My heart started pounding as my stomach sank and tears pricked the corner of my eyes.

"*What?*" I whispered, hoping I'd heard wrong.

"Yup," she said, sounding almost gleeful. "Told you he was a liar and a sleezeball. If you would have listened to me, you could have avoided all his shenanigans."

"I've gotta go, Mom. I love you and I'll see you later," I said quickly, needing to hang up before I said something I couldn't take back.

I sunk down onto the pretty iron bench Helen had set up in her flower garden on the side of the shop.

My ex-husband was having a baby with his new wife? The man who'd told me he didn't want to have more kids. Who said the ones he'd raised with his first wife were more than enough for him, even though he knew how much I'd wanted a baby?

"When is he going to stop hurting me?" I muttered quietly, willing the tears unsuccessfully not to fall.

I gave myself a few moments to mourn the life I'd wanted to have with Jared and then stood up and shook it off. Helen was counting on me to man the store while she took care of some personal business, and no one wanted to buy high-end clothing from a depressed woman with a tear-stained face.

I hurried inside, stopping in the bathroom to fix my makeup before going to relieve Helen at the front of the store.

"How's your mom feeling?" Helen asked when I joined her at the display.

"She said she's fine, but she didn't sound great. I'll go over there once Simone relieves me."

"I'll go see her this weekend."

"I'm sure she'll love that," I told Helen with a sunny smile. "Seeing you always makes her feel better."

"Okay, well, if you're all set here, I'm going to head out."

"You got it. I'll make sure the new stock gets loaded into the system and put out," I assured her.

I loved my job, and working with Helen was a dream. I got a great deal on beautiful clothes and jewelry and really enjoyed helping the customers find pieces that made them feel beautiful.

By the time Simone came in for the evening shift, I'd not only done everything I promised Helen I would, but I'd also updated the window display with some of our newest items. As I walked out of the shop for the night, I glanced at my handiwork and left with a smile on my face.

It felt wonderful to be satisfied in my work. Now if only my personal life could give me the same sense of contentment, I'd have everything I wanted.

I knew Whitney was probably busy with Luca and her kids, so I shot Margo a text asking if she'd be up for meeting for a drink. The thought of going back to my apartment, where I'd have to eat dinner alone and be stuck with my thoughts of Jared and Vanessa having a baby, was too unpleasant to imagine right now.

I unplugged my Audi e-tron GT and got behind the wheel.

The ridiculously expensive car was left over from my marriage, and if it was paid off, I'd totally sell it and keep the proceeds. But since Jared was currently paying on it, I'd happily keep driving it until the tires fell off.

I always felt silly parking it in my designated spot at my rundown apartment complex, which was the only thing I could currently afford, and often worried it wouldn't be there when I got up in the morning.

But so far, she was there every day. All pretty, shiny, and blue. My last token from my previous life.

The panel on my dashboard beeped and I looked over to see an incoming message from Margo.

I pressed play and it said, "Yeah, babe. I can meet you at Sullivan's in ten."

I knew I could count on Margo, I thought with a smile as I made a right toward the restaurant.

I used the valet. Grabbing my Louis Vuitton purse from the passenger side before getting out of the car, I gave the valet driver a flirty smile.

Okay, so I had more than one token left over from my marriage to Jared.

I felt lighter as I made my way inside to wait for Margo. Knowing I'd be seeing her made me feel a million times better than I had earlier, and I knew she'd help me sort through my feelings about Jared's new development.

I told the hostess we'd be a party of two and followed her through the room to an empty table near the bar.

Glancing around, I was about to take my seat when a familiar face snagged my attention. It took me a few moments to place him, but there was only one floppy-haired, sexy professor I'd been thinking about recently.

"*Noah*," I said out loud, not realizing *how* loud until Noah and the man he was sitting at the bar with both turned to look at me.

4

NOAH

"Wow, do you know her?" Trent asked, his tone reverent at the sight of the gorgeous woman who'd called out my name.

"No," I said, absolutely sure I'd never seen her before. *She's the kind of woman you'd remember meeting.* "She must be talking to someone else."

Her eyes widened and her cheeks turned pink before she seemed to jump into the chair and slide down as if she were trying to become invisible.

"Seems like she knows who you are," he said, turning his attention away from the woman to glance at me. "Are you holding out on me, man?"

I tore my eyes from the beautiful blonde and gave a derisive snort.

"Yeah, right," I muttered. "A woman like that wouldn't look twice at a guy like me. She can have anyone she wants."

"A truer statement has never been spoken, but I swear she looked at you like you were the last slice of chocolate cake on the planet."

"You're the only person I know with a chocolate cake obsession. I'm sure she was simply embarrassed because she thought I was someone else."

"Whoa, check out the woman who just joined her. I swear women weren't this hot when I was single," Trent said, looking indiscreetly over his shoulder. "Except for Cam, of course."

"Of course," I mimicked with a grin. If there was ever a man who would do anything for his wife, it was Trent. Still, he loved to act like being married was a chore and he missed the single life. Since I knew him when he was single, I knew it was all bullshit. Trent had never been happier.

I shifted so I could check out the table and see what he was going on about.

A very tall, sleek, and I'd have to say, intimidating as hell, woman had joined the blonde, who I also found intimidating, but in a different way. The raven-haired woman looked like she would literally take a man by the balls and have him do her bidding, while the petite blonde had the whole Marilyn Monroe thing going on.

To put it simply, I had no business even looking in their direction.

I fumbled absently with the button on my cuff and noticed I'd gotten some wing sauce on my sleeve.

"Of course I did," I mumbled, before flagging down the bartender. "Can I get another draft and some club soda, please?"

"Another one?" he asked Trent, who shook his head and said, "Better not."

"Cam still got you on that diet?" I asked when it was the two of us again.

Trent sighed and looked longingly at the remains of my wings.

"It feels like we're always trying a new diet. First it was Atkins, then the Mediterranean diet ... the whole thirty, paleo, Nutrisystem ... If it's out there, we've tried it. I wish we could just eat what we want to eat and be happy."

"Have you told Cam that?" I asked, grateful I didn't have anyone monitoring my food intake.

I'm sure my late-night gummy worm addiction wouldn't be a big hit with most ladies.

"Nah. Ever since Cam had Tucker, she's been self-conscious about the baby weight. I'm trying to be supportive by dieting with her. I just wish she saw herself the way I see her. I mean, she's perfect, ya know?"

I nodded in solidarity and then my gaze wandered back to the table behind us, as if of their own volition.

"They're looking over here," I whispered to Trent, nerves suddenly flooding my body. "Holy shit, the dark-haired one is getting up ... she's staring at us ... she's coming over ... *be cool*."

The last was said in kind of a whisper-shout as I shifted in my seat to face straight forward, my back going rigid as all the reasons she could be coming over ran through my mind.

Did she catch us staring? Think we were creeps? Is she pissed her friend had gotten embarrassed?

"Well ... hello, professor," she said, her tone playful, yet somehow stern.

Wondering how the hell she knew where we worked, I turned with a curious expression.

"To which professor are you referring?" I asked, wincing when I could hear the stodginess in my voice.

"Oh, are you both studious, then?" she asked with a smirk.

Trent just looked up at her, his mouth slightly agape.

"Yes, ma'am," I replied. "Can we help you with something?"

"You're Noah, right?" she asked, causing me to give her a baffled nod. "I'm Margo, and that bombshell over there is my friend, Summer."

"Uh, this is Trent," I replied automatically, even though I couldn't for the life of me figure out what the hell was going on.

"Hello, Trent," Margo said, turning to look at him for the first time. She seemed to look him over, before her gaze landed on his left hand. "Hmm, married. Pity."

I wanted to laugh at my friend's stunned expression, but I was too confused.

"How do I know you?" I asked when she turned her attention back to me.

"You don't. But my friend saw you on that True Love dating app."

I flushed as her words registered. I'd joined that app on a dare from Trent. I hadn't been on it in over a year and hadn't realized my profile was still active.

"Oh, no, sorry, I meant to close that account," I said hurriedly.

"So, you're no longer single?" she asked, one eyebrow winging up.

"He's definitely single," Trent put in before I could reply.

I shot him a look before asking, "Why? Did you guys have a friend you wanted to set me up with or something?"

It seemed far-fetched, but the fact that she was standing there talking to me was against the laws of nature, so anything was possible.

"Summer, actually," Margo said, gesturing back to her friend. "She saw you on the app, but accidently pressed the wrong button and couldn't contact you."

I blinked rapidly, like ten times, looking at Summer, who was blushing furiously as she sucked her beverage through a straw, then back at Margo.

"Her?" I asked, the question coming out a bit harsher than I intended. "And *me*? You can't be serious."

"I'm always serious," Margo said, her face going a little scary. "Are you saying you aren't interested?"

I scoffed and said, "I'm saying I think you must be mistaken. I don't think I'm your friend's type."

Her eyes narrowed as she took in my stained sleeve, loose button, and the tweed jacket on the back of my stool.

"I'm going to give you the benefit of the doubt and assume

you're ignorant to your own charms, rather than insinuating that Summer isn't good enough for you."

"What? *No ... I mean, yes ... er, no*. I would never say *she* wasn't good enough for *me*. She's obviously gorgeous," I stuttered, while Trent looked at me, his eyes pleading with me to *shut the hell up*.

"Great," Margo said, holding out her hand. "Give me your phone and I'll program in her number. You're obviously flustered, so take a few days and work up the nerve, then give her a call. What's the harm in one date, right? You never know what could happen."

I handed her my phone, too afraid to object, then accepted it back with a "Thank you."

When she walked away, I turned to Trent and asked, "What the hell just happened?"

"I think you just won the lottery, man."

5

SUMMER

He hadn't called.

After Margo had left me at our table to go and talk with Noah and his friend, I'd almost died of embarrassment.

I could only imagine the things Margo was saying as I willed myself, unsuccessfully, to become invisible.

I was normally a confident woman. I'd been told all my life that I was beautiful and even when I was only sixteen, grown men had stopped me on the street to say often-inappropriate things.

But I knew being attractive wasn't the kind of thing that would endear me to a man like Noah. In fact, in my less-than-vast experience, I found men like him as intimidated by me as I was by them.

It was as irrational as a person being afraid of a tiny spider. We knew in our minds that there was nothing to fear, we were all only human, after all, but there was something either in our genetic makeup or the way we were raised that made us think we were ill suited for each other.

I had been called, many times, I may add ... a *trophy wife*. According to the Urban Dictionary: A Trophy Wife was defined as *a young, attractive woman married to an older, more powerful man. His role in the relationship is to be her sugar daddy and provide her with power and material things.*

In other words, I was arm candy at best.

I didn't like thinking of myself in this way, and when I'd first heard a woman at my ex-husband's yacht club call me that, I was devastated. Even though I could see how technically it was true. My husband was older and he'd also had a lot of money. But I'd married him because I loved him, and I'd believed in us. I also knew I had more to offer the world than simply my looks, so I took offense and hadn't befriended those nasty women.

They'd acted like I'd done them a favor. Because why would they want to be friends with a woman like me? The kind of woman who stole husbands.

Being a sensitive person, I'd been hurt at first, but eventually I learned to ignore them and built a wall around my heart. It wasn't until I met Whitney and Margo that I found women who saw me for who I was and didn't slap a label on me and call it quits.

I still understood that a man like Noah probably saw my outer package and tucked me away in a box in his mind that considered me not only unattainable, but unsuitable.

I'd hoped after Margo told me about their conversation and that she'd given him my number, that he'd be different. But apparently, I'd been wrong. I couldn't deny it stung a bit and I was allowing myself to have a little pity party over it.

That was why I was in yoga pants and a sweatshirt, wearing no makeup with my hair up in a messy bun, perusing the aisle of ice cream in my local grocery store.

Rocky Road, Mint Chocolate Chip, Chunky Monkey ... the possibilities are endless, and right now, they all sound so good.

I opened the glass door and started picking out pints and dropping them into my hand-held basket. They would all keep in the freezer; it wasn't as if I'd actually eat them *all* tonight.

Once my basket was heavy and full of ice cream, I closed the door and turned to head toward the front of the store to check out. I stopped cold when I saw Noah standing at the end of the aisle, peering through the glass.

My first instinct was to turn and flee. Instead, I held my heavy basket with two hands and tiptoed slowly over to where he was standing.

Maybe he'd leave before I got there...

When I was a few steps away, I cleared my throat and called, "Noah?"

He turned his head, looking momentarily puzzled before he started blinking rapidly and dropped what he'd been holding.

Automatically, I crouched down to pick up the bag of frozen strawberries. Unfortunately, so did he, and our heads bumped together before we both pulled back.

"*Oh, no*! I'm so sorry," Noah mumbled, grabbing the strawberries and thrusting them back into the freezer before standing to look down at me while absently rubbing his forehead. "Are you okay?"

"Yes, just a little tap. No worries," I assured him with a sunny grin. When he continued to watch me with his soft brown eyes, but didn't say anything further, I said, "It's Summer ... from the other night. You talked with my friend, Margo."

"Yes, of course. I remember. Uh, how are you?" he asked, rocking slowly side to side.

"I'd be better if you called," I replied, hoping it came across as flirty rather than accusing.

"Yeah, well, I..." he started, running a hand through his hair, and letting out a nervous laugh. "I wasn't sure you really wanted me to."

"Yes," I said, a little too quickly. "I did ... *do* ... want you to. Everything Margo said to you is a hundred percent true. I totally would have tried to contact you through the app, if my fat fingers hadn't hit the wrong button."

I held up my hand, as if to show him evidence of my fat fingers, and then remembered how I looked.

"*Oh my gosh*, I look terrible," I whispered, stepping back and raising my hand to shift the bun on top of my head, suddenly horrified. I couldn't believe I'd actually approached him with no makeup on.

"Are you kidding? You look gorgeous," Noah scoffed, before seeming to realize what he said and sucking his lips into his mouth as he shook his head and shut his eyes.

Pleasure filled me at his words and his reaction assured me they were the truth.

I giggled and he opened one eye to peer down at me.

"Thank you. That's very sweet."

Noah shrugged sheepishly and said, "You have to know how beautiful you are, regardless of what you're wearing to dress it up."

I wanted to throw my arms around him and hug him tightly; instead I looked up at him and asked, "So, will you please call? Or you can text, that works, too."

"I'm not much of a texter and I know as soon as you walk away, I'll lose the nerve to call," he admitted, causing my floating heart to deflate a bit. "So, I would rather just ask you now." Noah cleared his throat and asked formally, "Would you like to go dancing with me on Friday night?"

"Dancing?" I asked, completely surprised. Dancing was the last thing I'd expected him to want to do. "Yes, I'd love to. What time?"

"I can pick you up at nine, if that works."

"How about you text me the address and I'll meet you there at nine?" I countered. I may have had a crush on him, but I didn't actually know him, and I never let strangers pick me up at my house. I was too cautious for that.

"That works, too," Noah said easily.

"Great," I said with a grin. "I can't wait until Friday!"

I gave him a little finger wave and turned, being sure to put a little extra swing in my hips as I walked. When I was about halfway down the aisle, I turned to look over my shoulder, and when I saw him standing in the same spot, holding those strawberries again, his eyes on me, I blew him a jaunty kiss.

When Noah dropped the bag of strawberries, I let out a delighted laugh and left him to go purchase my ice cream.

6

NOAH

"There's a precious girl. *Coochie coochie coo*," I murmured to my three-month-old niece as I rocked with her in an old wooden chair.

"Dude, don't talk to her like she's an idiot," my brother, Charles, said as he walked into the room holding two beers.

"It's baby talk," I argued, glancing worriedly down at Suzy's sweet, innocent face. "You know I don't think you're an idiot. You're going to be a genius."

"I'm just saying, you don't have to hit her with the baby talk. Simply talk to her like you would anyone else."

"I don't understand," I said as he placed a bottle on the table next to me and then sat down on the sofa. "You want me to talk to her as if she understands what I'm saying?"

"Yes. Jamilla has read some studies about it and apparently it helps with their cognitive development. I don't know ... she's the expert. But if she hears you doing that coochie shit she's gonna bop you upside the head."

Jamilla was a child life specialist and one of the smartest women I knew, so if she believed I should talk to Suzy as if she were an adult, then that's what I'd do. She was the subject matter expert, after all.

"What brought you by?" Charles asked as he relaxed into the couch. "Not that I don't always love to see you, big brother, but you're not usually the drop-in type."

"Well," I began, suddenly too embarrassed to explain to him why I was there.

It was sad that my younger brother was the person I was going to for relationship advice. It should be the other way around, but that had never been our dynamic. Charles had always been the extrovert. The *charming, handsome, always ready with a smile, big man on campus* type. While I was more your, *reading in the library during lunch, debate team, please don't talk to me* type.

This had actually really worked for me during college. I'd gone to University of Texas at Austin, and once there, I'd found like-minded souls and a community of enrichment.

"Uh-oh, you're stalling. Must be something good," Charles said with an easy grin. "Come on. You know you can say anything to me."

I nodded because I did know that. Charles was one of my best friends and the most honorable person I knew, besides our father, of course.

I cleared my throat and said, "There's this woman..."

Charles leaned forward and rested his elbows on his thighs.

"Go on..."

"She's, ah ... well, she's gorgeous. I'm talking beautiful face, ridiculous body, and this charming disposition, which really should make the entire combination illegal. I have no idea how she's single, or why she's interested in *me*, but apparently that's the case."

"Wow, do you have a picture?" he asked, causing me to scowl at him.

"How would I have a picture? I don't go around snapping shots of beautiful strangers. That's creepy."

Charles laughed easily and asked, "How'd you meet?"

Suzy let out a belch and when I looked down, she had white stuff coming out of her mouth.

"Is this normal?" I asked, worried.

"Yeah, here," my brother said, reaching over to grab a white cloth out of a basket on the table and handing it to me.

I very gently wiped the curd-looking stuff off of her face, and when she closed her eyes, I settled back into the chair and resumed rocking.

"What were we saying?" I asked, distracted.

"You were telling me how you met this amazing woman."

"Oh," I stated absently, and then proceeded to tell him about our encounters at the bar and the grocery store.

"You're right, she certainly is into you."

"It's weird, right?" I said with a slight shrug. "It seems to go against nature, but there you have it. She's been in a sort of active pursuit. It throws me off. But I did set up a date for Friday night."

"What are you planning to do?"

"Well, I figured dinner and a movie would be too basic for a woman like her, right? And there are so many other possibilities where I would not end up in a positive light, so I figured why not do something I'm good at, so at least I'll feel confident, even if I'm nervous about being on a date with her."

"So..."

"Dancing."

Charles blinked and then grinned. "Is that what you told her? You were taking her dancing?"

"Yeah. Why?" I asked.

"Well, we live in the city. She's a gorgeous, polished woman, who is single and sexy, and you said you were taking her dancing."

"So?"

"So, lug head, she probably expects you to take her to a club."

"A club?" I asked, horrified by the prospect.

"Yeah, man. *A club.* I bet you a hundred dollars that's what she expects." Charles chuckled and slapped his knee. "I wish I could be a fly on the wall when you show up at a country bar ready to show her how well you can two-step."

"I won a contest in college," I murmured.

"Yeah, *I know*," he said, rolling his eyes.

"You really think she expects me to take her out dancing at a nightclub? Should I text her and tell her? I mean, when I give her the address of where to meet me, she'll see what kind of place it is."

"Yeah, you're probably right. Still, I mean it about the hundred bucks. I'm gonna go grab a beer, you need?"

I glanced at the untouched bottle next to me and shook my head.

When he walked out of the room, I looked down at my niece and asked, "What do you think, Sooz? Will she be disappointed by line dancing?"

Suzy opened her eyes and blinked at me.

Thinking of Charles' earlier words, I shifted to reach in my pocket and pulled out my pocket-sized copy of *Love Sonnets of Shakespeare* and began to read aloud. I'd do whatever I could to help my niece's cognitive development.

7
SUMMER

"Oh my gosh, this has felt like the longest week," I said as I threw my purse to the floor and sat down at the table.

It was Thursday night, so Whitney, Margo, and I were meeting for dinner and drinks. Tonight, Margo had picked a hip new tapas place.

"It really has," Whitney agreed.

"Why am I always the last one here? I swear I try to leave early to beat you guys, but it never seems to work out."

Margo simply smiled and lifted her drink at me.

They were used to my perpetual lateness.

"Anyway, I've been *dying* to see you guys. I feel like it's been *ages* since last Thursday."

Whitney nodded enthusiastically, which was weird for her. In fact, she looked like she was about to explode.

"Are you okay?" I asked, suddenly concerned.

She nodded and bit her lip, then thrust out her left hand.

It took a moment for me to realize I was supposed to look at it, since I was searching her face for a hint at what was happening. When I heard Margo say, "*Hell, yeah*," I glanced down and couldn't miss the giant, dazzling diamond on her finger.

"*No*," I gasped, reaching for her hand and practically yanking her out of her chair as I pulled the ring closer. "When ... how ... *when*?"

"Sunday," Whitney managed, the word coming out choked.

"*Sunday*?" I screeched. "And you're just telling us now?"

"I wanted to tell you in person. Believe me. These have been the longest four days of my life," she said with a watery laugh.

"*Whitney*," I scolded. "This is the type of thing that warrants an emergency meeting! If you'd called, we'd have come over anytime, day or night."

"I'm sure she needed time to process, Summer. It's a big deal," Margo said, eyeing the ring warily as if it may be contagious.

"What's done is done," I said with a wave of my hand, before catching Whit's eyes and pleading, "Tell us everything."

"He did it at Sunday dinner, with Si and Stella, and his whole family around. It was sweet and emotional, and perfect." Tears spilled over and I handed her a napkin. "Luca got down on one knee, and his mom started to cry. He asked me and then he asked Stella and Si if they'd accept him as a permanent part of their lives. It was unexpected and just, everything I didn't know I wanted. *I'm so happy...*"

She wept softly and I held her hand, smiling so hard my cheeks hurt.

"You deserve it, Whit," Margo said, reaching over to pat her on the shoulder. "Congratulations."

"Thank you," she managed.

"Have you already started on the details?" I asked, practically vibrating with excitement at the prospect of a wedding.

"Well, I tried to say I wanted something small and unassuming, but was immediately vetoed," Whit said with a chuckle. "There's no way Luca's mother was going to let me get away with that. And I get it. Luca hasn't been married before and his family is massive. They want to celebrate."

"Yay! I mean, I'm sorry you don't get your small affair, but I'm so happy you're going to do a big wedding."

"You would be," Margo joked dryly.

I punched her softly in the arm and she winked in response.

"I put my foot down about the dress. I'm not standing up for a second time in a big puffy number. I want something simple, elegant, and *not* white. Stella will be my maid of honor and Silas, one of Luca's groomsmen, and I'll walk myself down the aisle."

I waited patiently, hoping I knew what she was going to say next, my leg jiggling anxiously under the table.

"And I'd love it if the two of you would be bridesmaids."

"Yes," I shouted gleefully, while Margo stated much more softly, "Of course."

We ordered champagne to celebrate and chatted about the wedding over tapas.

When things were winding down, Margo asked, "Did you tell Whit about Noah?"

"Who's Noah?" Whitney asked.

"Remember the professor on the dating app who I accidentally deleted?"

"Yeah."

"Well, he was at the same bar as Margo and me the other night."

"No way, really?" she asked with a smile. "How did that go?"

"Margo scared the crap out of him and gave him my number."

Whitney shot Margo an amused glance.

"It's true. He was scared," Margo said with a laugh. "But totally sweet and absentminded. Absolutely Summer's type." She turned my way and asked, "Did he call?"

"No. But I ran into him at the grocery store and confronted him about it."

"I would have loved to see that," Margo said with a grin. "I bet he didn't know what to do. Good for you."

"We're going out tomorrow night," I told them, so excited I could barely contain the words.

"Whoa, way to bury the lead. I can't believe you held that in so long."

I nodded at Whitney, because I too was surprised I held on to the information and hadn't spit it out as soon as I'd sat, but her engagement took precedence and I'd wanted to share in her excitement before turning the focus to mine.

"We're going dancing. I found the perfect dress at the shop and I'm getting a blow out tomorrow afternoon."

"I bet he'll be speechless when he sees you in your club getup," Margo said with a sly grin.

We'd gone out plenty, so she'd seen me at my most, or least, dressed. I didn't want to scare Noah away, so I wasn't going to look quite so promiscuous, but the dress was short, and tight, and I hoped he'd feel something when he saw me in it.

Specifically in his pants.

Chemistry was a key element to any successful relationship. I knew I felt it when I was with him, and I was going to do everything in my power to make sure he felt it too.

8

NOAH

I'd been so anxious for this date that I'd had a stomachache for days. And now that it was time to actually meet up with Summer, I was in a complete tizzy.

Yes, that was an expression more suited to the baby boomer generation, but it was an apt description of how I was feeling.

I'd gotten to the country bar a half an hour early. I didn't want to be late, and if she happened to come early, I didn't want her to have to wait outside alone. So, I'd figured the best course of action was to get there with plenty of time to spare.

When it was fifteen minutes after we were supposed to meet, I began to worry she wasn't going to show.

Had the whole thing been an elaborate ruse? Was someone punking me, for lack of a better term? And if so, who and why? I couldn't think of anyone I'd angered or anyone who hated me so much they'd want to see me suffer humiliation, but the world was an often times cruel place.

I waged a war within myself ... to stay or to leave.

On one hand, if it was a joke on me, then the longer I stayed, the more ammunition I gave my would-be tormenter.

On the other, if my imagination had once again gotten the

better of me and she was simply late, I'd feel horrible if she arrived after I'd left.

So, I stayed.

At twenty minutes after the hour, an Audi came squealing into the parking lot and I watched as Summer emerged from the driver's seat as if she were a mermaid breaking the surface.

Encased in a form-fitting, short dress with a plunging neckline in a mossy green that I knew would complement her eyes perfectly, she looked like a goddess ready to meet her match.

As I stepped from the shadows in my cowboy boots and Levi's, I felt unworthy and woefully out of my league. When Summer's gaze landed on me, her face blossomed with a happy smile and her eyes seemed to sparkle with excitement.

It was enough to bring a fool to his knees.

"Noah," she called with an exuberant wave.

Her guileless behavior was in such contrast to her definitively womanly appearance that it made me yearn to learn what made this gorgeous creature tick. I'd definitely never met anyone like her before, and I found myself utterly intrigued by her.

"You look amazing," I managed, accepting her outstretched hands and holding them briefly.

"I'm so sorry I'm late. I swear, I try my best to be early, or at the very least on time, but it never seems to work out that way," Summer said sheepishly. "I was having a hard time getting my hair right."

I looked at her hair, and although I thought it looked the same as always, I was a smart enough man not to say so. Instead, I said, "Well worth the wait."

Summer beamed at me before glancing over at the neon lights of the bar.

"I've never been here before."

I fought a wince and replied, "It's a country and western bar. After speaking with my brother, I realized I should have explained that when I asked you to come dancing, I meant line-dancing and two-stepping."

Summer's mouth formed an "o" and some of her excitement dropped away.

"I've never been. I hope I don't embarrass you."

"Impossible," I assured her. "And I'm a pretty good teacher. I promise you'll get the hang of things in no time, and if you find you don't like it, we don't have to stay. Deal?"

"Deal," she said easily, showing me another side of herself.

I was finding a new facet to Summer with each interaction and, so far, I liked them all.

I offered her my hand and she took it with a smile, so I led her inside and watched her face as the atmosphere hit her.

Low lights, wood as far as the eye could see, and rustic décor. This place was the closest thing to Texas I'd been able to find, with the country music blaring and the peanuts on the dining room floor.

The dance floor was crowded with people dancing along to the latest trend and the scent in the air was a mixture of grilled beef and beer.

I loved everything about it, and when Summer's face broke into an excited grin, I knew she was ready to embrace the evening.

"You want a drink? Maybe something to eat?" I asked, leaning down to speak close to her ear since it was so loud inside.

"A drink would be good," she replied, so I bypassed the dining area and walked toward the long bar, lined with barstools and decorated with beer bottle tops.

Summer hopped up into one of the chairs, causing her already short dress to slide farther up, giving me a glorious view of tanned, toned skin. It was enough to have my pulse racing and an internal struggle where I forced myself to tear my gaze away from the view.

I cleared my throat as I settled onto the stool and searched desperately for the bartender.

When he came over and asked what he could get us, Summer

said, "Margarita, please," while I practically begged, "Whatever you have on tap is fine."

I was suddenly parched.

Summer chatted happily about the décor and how much she was enjoying the music. She didn't seem phased at all that she was surrounded by people in jeans, cowboy boots, and plaid, or the fact that the women's looks were tinged with jealousy, while the men's were downright lascivious.

She was a beacon in the darkened room, and I found myself mesmerized by the way her deep green eyes seemed to pull me in and how the tinkle of her laugh made me feel.

From everything I'd seen so far, she was as beautiful inside as she was out, and for whatever reason, she was here tonight with me. It was surreal, and I vowed to enjoy every second of it, for however long it lasted.

9

SUMMER

I was having *the best* time.

The night hadn't gone at all like I'd expected when I'd gotten ready and left my apartment. In fact, it was even better.

Noah was obviously in his comfort zone. He was smiling, laughing, and dancing his heart out. It was super sweet and a completely different side of him. He was confident in his skin and his skills, and it was well-founded.

At first when he'd asked me to dance the two-step to a slow song, I'd been game, but a little nervous. I didn't want to embarrass myself by stepping on his feet or stumbling around, but the second his hands touched my body, I'd relaxed.

He was a strong leader and had maneuvered me around the dance floor effortlessly.

I had to admit, it was extremely sexy.

His natural prowess, coupled with the feel of his large, strong hands on me, had made the dance an intensely arousing experience.

Plus, it was fun. Line dancing, two-stepping, and talking over drinks at the bar.

"This is one of the best dates I've been on in forever," I told him happily as we both threw back some water in an effort to stay hydrated. "Maybe ever."

Noah's smile was pleased, and I thought his cheeks may have even pinked a bit at my admission.

"Me, too," he replied sweetly, making my heart turn over in my chest. "You're really easy to be around."

"You sound surprised."

He gave a half shrug and said, "Well, in my limited experience, women like you..."

"Yes?" I prodded when he didn't finish his thought.

"I don't want to offend you."

"You won't," I assured him. "I have a pretty thick skin."

"Why's that?" Noah asked, his gaze curious.

"Are you avoiding answering?"

He chuckled and said, "Busted. No, I was going to say, women who look like you are often high maintenance and wouldn't necessarily look at me, and a date like this, and feel satisfied with their choice. *Sorry*," he added with a wince.

I laughed easily.

"That's not offensive at all. Believe me, I have been around plenty of women like that, but I'm not like that. I like to say, I'm the exception to the rule ... you can't judge me by my cover."

The worry cleared and he nodded.

"I like that a lot," he said. "Now, I answered ... your turn."

I looked up at him and nodded, then asked, "Want to grab a table? I would kill for some fries right now."

"Sure." He grabbed our drinks off of the bar and led me back to the dining area and grabbed the last free table.

Once we were seated and the harried server took our order, fries for me and a burger and fries for Noah, I answered his question.

"I'd say my thick skin is two-fold. I won't go into too much detail, because I don't want to ruin what has so far been a super-fun night." When he nodded, I continued, "I had an older sister, who I don't remember. She died when I was three

... she needed surgery and there was a complication at the hospital ... anyway, the next year my father left. He couldn't deal with the loss of my sister and my mom's subsequent depression. I haven't seen him since, and my mom never really got over it, so it felt like I raised her more than she raised me." I lifted a shoulder and thanked the server for my fries. Once I'd drowned them in ketchup, I picked one up and took a bite. "Yum!"

"I'm so sorry. That's a lot to go through at such a young age," Noah said kindly as he dressed his burger.

"Luckily, I had Helen, my mom's best friend since high school. She was the one who took me back-to-school shopping and talked to me about boys. She's the reason I fell in love with fashion. I manage her boutique ... I guess you could say she was more of a mom to me than my own mother, although I'd never tell my mom that."

"It's good you had someone. I'd hate to think of you basically growing up alone."

"It wasn't all bad," I said, suddenly feeling guilty for talking about my mother. "My mom had good days and it's not her fault her heart was broken."

Noah nodded, and I think he could sense my guilt and that I didn't want to talk about my childhood anymore, because he asked, "What's the second part?"

I sighed, knowing this part often made me look like a bad person, but decided I wanted to be a hundred percent honest with Noah. I really liked him so far, and if he had any chance of getting to see if he felt the same, he needed to know the truth.

"When I was in my mid-twenties, after college, when I was just starting out with Helen, I met Jared. He was older ... twenty-years older and seemed to have it all. He was lavish with his attention, and gifts, and he really swept me off my feet. I fell head over heels in love and then when we were on vacation in the south of France, he told me he was married. I was devastated. Not only because he lied, but because he'd made me into a cheater, something I'd sworn to never be. He assured me he was leaving her and that he loved me and wanted to marry me..."

Noah nodded, but I wondered if the look on his face meant I'd lost some of my sparkle in his eyes.

"And he did. Divorce her and marry me ... so I convinced myself it was all okay, since we were in love. Sure, I got the look from his friends and their wives called me Jared's trophy wife, but I thought it would work. Then he told me he didn't want to have more children. His kids with his ex-wife were now adults and he didn't want to start over. I was devastated, but loved him, so, I figured I'd get over it. Then he did the same thing to me he'd done to his ex ... cheated, divorced me, and married her. Now they're having a baby."

I took a sip of my fresh margarita and looked at him to see his reaction. I hoped he wasn't disgusted.

"Wow," he said after a few beats. "That's a lot. I can understand why you'd have thick skin after everything you've been through."

"Thanks. And I know it's like against first date rules to talk about your ex, but I wanted to be upfront and honest with you. I really like you, Noah, and I hope you'll like me too, even after hearing about all my baggage."

Noah's lips turned up. "Everyone has baggage, Summer. It doesn't reflect negatively on you, it's simply what happened to make you into the woman you are today."

"What's your baggage?"

He chuckled and said, "Well, embarrassingly enough, I guess I don't really have any. My parents are still together. They're both retired. My dad was a professor, like me, and my mom was a curator. My younger brother, Charles, is married and has a baby. I love my work and my family and friends. I guess you could say the fact that I'm still single, even though I've always wanted a family, would be the only downside in my life."

"So, no skeletons then?"

"I'm afraid not."

"That's okay. I probably have enough for both of us," I joked.

We finished our food and decided to call it a night, since it was already after one in the morning.

Noah walked me to my car, and I had a feeling he was going to be a perfect gentleman and not move in for a kiss.

Since my body was still all a-tingle from being in close proximity and being in his arms most of the night, and I loved kissing more than almost anything in the world, I decided to take control of the situation and go for what I wanted.

When he was about to turn to go, I touched his arm to stop him, then launched myself at him. It was a bit like scaling a tree, but once I got my arms around his neck, he helped me out by dipping his head down.

His lips were full and soft, and when they parted and our mouths were fused, magic happened. It was everything I loved about kissing all at once. Soft, warm, excited, and full of spark.

I let a soft moan of pleasure loose, which seemed to be all the encouragement Noah needed. He deepened the kiss, his hands coming to my ass to grab and lift, until my legs were around his waist, and I was braced back against my car.

Ohhhh, it was fabulous. Sweet turned hot, with a lot of grinding in between.

It went on a deliciously long time, until Noah eventually broke away and gently placed me back on my feet.

"Goodnight," I said dreamily.

He looked a little stunned, but managed to say, "Drive safe," before walking in a zig-zag pattern back to his car.

A laugh escaped my lips as I got in my car and drove home, and I didn't stop smiling until I fell asleep.

Maybe not even then.

10

NOAH

"Dear, can you take out the drink cart? Your father asked me, but I need to take these tartlets out of the oven."

"Sure," I said, crossing the kitchen to open the door to the butler's pantry. It was the third Sunday of the month, which meant my parents' monthly book club meeting. I stopped by when I could, and when they were discussing a book I'd read, which was most of the time.

I pushed the stocked cart out into the formal living room, where my father and his friends were gathered. As soon as they saw me enter, they attacked, as if the bourbon was a fresh kill and they a pack of feral animals.

I got out of the way as fast as possible and went back into the kitchen to help my mother.

It was often the case that while my father was sneaking outside to smoke cigars in between book points, my mother and I would stay in the kitchen and drink tea. I'd always been close with both of my parents, but my mother and I had a special bond.

"Need help with anything else?" I asked as she plated the tarts.

"You can put the sandwiches on the tiered serving stand."

I moved to the cupboard with the platters and serving dishes and pulled out the stand, then began piling the cut sandwiches on it.

"So, how was your week? Anything exciting happen at work?" she asked as we worked.

"Not really, just the usual," I said, mentally debating whether or not I should bring up my date with Summer. I didn't date often, and when I did, I usually told my parents about it. They never got too overbearing about it, like I'd seen some parents do ... always asking when their kids would get married and give them grandchildren, even before Charles checked those boxes.

They were simply interested in my life, and I enjoyed discussing everything with them.

But for some reason talking about Summer felt different. Important somehow. And I was uncharacteristically nervous about bringing her up.

We took the food to the living room and arranged it neatly on the oversized antique coffee table. The guys knew to wait until my mother had arranged everything to her liking and got out of the way, before they pounced.

The room was filled with their excited chatter as we exited.

Once we were back in the kitchen, my mother picked up a serving tray filled with snacks and tea for us and took it to the breakfast nook.

When we were both seated and she began serving the tea, she gave me a pointed look and asked, "Well, are you ready to tell me what's on your mind?"

I brought my eyes to hers, unsurprised by her intuition and forthrightness.

"I met a woman," I began, pausing because I was still uncertain what exactly I wanted to say ... or admit.

"How lovely," she said as she added two lumps of sugar to her tea. "Did you meet her at the university?"

"No, actually," I said with a chuckle. "It's this convoluted story about a dating app Trent signed me up for and a chance meeting at a bar. A meet-cute if you will."

"Oh, I love that. What's she like?"

I picked up a fruit tart, *my favorite*, and thought about Summer.

"Summer is ... well, as her name implies," I began, picturing her as I spoke. "She's warm, bright, and smells just like she's been sun kissed. She gives every indication of having a good, kind heart, and she's quick to smile."

"You're smiling now," my mom said, pulling me from my thoughts.

"What?"

"While you're talking about her. I've never seen you smile in quite that way," she said, her own lips turning up as she observed, "You're smitten."

"What?" I asked with an embarrassed laugh. "No, I'm not ... I'm not a schoolgirl, after all. I simply find her attractive and enjoy her company."

"Hmmm, I don't know. That's a new expression on you. I hope we'll get to meet her..."

That had me blinking as visions of Summer left and I took in my mother's steady gaze.

"I've only recently met her myself. We're not anywhere near the *meeting each other's parents'* stage, if we ever get there," I protested.

"Why wouldn't you?" she asked.

"Well, for one thing it's been ages since I was serious about anyone enough to bring them to family functions." My mother nodded in agreement. "And for another, she's different than any woman I've ever dated. I'm not sure she'd want to end up with a guy like me, but I'm going to enjoy being with her for as long as I can."

"That doesn't sound like you. You're a wonderful man and any woman would be extremely lucky to end up with you as a husband. It's also not fair to Summer. It seems you're labeling her and putting her in a box on a shelf, when you should be open to giving the relationship a chance and seeing where it goes."

"Mom, she's gorgeous. Like, out-of-this-world, supermodel gorgeous," I said, inadvertently smiling again as her likeness popped back in my mind. "She's in fashion and has a car that costs more than I make annually."

"I'm an artist who fell in love with a professor, and I made more than your father," she said, arching an eyebrow at me like she did when she thought I was being foolish. "Opposites attract, you know, and often make the best partners. What do you have in common?"

"Not our families, or the way we were brought up. Not our past relationships ... I don't know, we don't know everything about each other. But we do both want to have a family, get married and have kids."

"That's a great start."

Eager to change the subject to something besides me and Summer, I asked, "So, what about you? Anything fun happen this week?"

She shot me a look that said she knew what I was doing, but her face blossomed as she said, "I watched Suzy yesterday. It was glorious."

Perfect. There was nothing my mother loved more than talking about her only grandchild. I was sure she'd regale me with tales of baby smiles and all of Suzy's stunning attributes until it was time for me to join the men for a rousing discussion of John Grisham's novel.

II

SUMMER

Noah hadn't been lying, he wasn't much of a texter.

After a few failed attempts to reach him that way, I'd finally bit the bullet and called him. He'd answered on the first ring, and we'd talked well into the night. Since then, I'd made it a habit to give him a call every few days. It didn't always result in a long conversation, sometimes just a quick hello, but in doing so I'd been able to suggest another date, this time lunch during the week.

We'd both been really busy with work and other obligations, so hadn't been able to get together any other time. And after the way we'd left things, I'd been dying to see him again and see if our chemistry had been a fluke, or if we'd still have it in the light of day.

I'd agreed to meet him at a place by the university, since his break was shorter than mine, and had been waiting at a table by the window. I was so excited to see him again, I'd arrived about fifteen minutes early.

As I usually did whenever I had extra time, I'd pulled out my sketchbook and began to draw to pass the time.

I'd started fooling around with a few ideas I had for Whitney's wedding dress and had about a dozen pages so far. I knew she didn't want anything elaborate, so I'd been playing with simple lines, going for elegant and a variety of tones ranging from eggshell to an elegant champagne.

"Oh, no, am I late?" Noah said, his words coming out in a rush as he sat across from me. "I was helping a student ... I hope you haven't been waiting long."

I put down my pencil and shut my book before looking up at him with an easy smile. I drank him in as I took in his face. He was really so handsome, and I loved the way he brushed his hair off of his forehead as he got settled.

"You're right on time," I assured him.

"Good, good," he replied, seeming ruffled over my beating him to the restaurant. "I'd hate to think I kept you."

"It's good to see you," I said, hoping to ease his worry.

Noah took a breath, and after his gaze landed on my face, he seemed to settle.

"You, too. I'm sorry we haven't been able to get together before this, but as we near finals, the students in all of my classes start to panic." Noah chuckled and ran his fingers through his hair. "Everyone wants extra study sessions and makeup work and I do my best to accommodate them."

"That's very sweet of you. I'm sure most professors wouldn't be so understanding."

"Well, I want them to succeed. They're paying good money to take my classes and I want to do everything possible to help them. Sure, there are those who don't put in the time or effort to do well, and there's really nothing I can do for them. But if there's a student who is willing to put in the time and do the work, then I'll do whatever I can to help."

He's so wonderful, I thought as he took glasses out of his pocket and put them on before picking up his menu.

I mimicked the movement, trying not to notice how sexy he looked in those glasses.

I'd already perused the menu and knew what I wanted, but if I didn't do something, I'd sit there staring at him like a lovesick puppy, and I didn't want to do that. As soon as we put our menus down, the server came over to take our orders and then left us to go and put them in.

"What do you have there?" Noah asked, nodding toward my sketchbook as he shrugged out of his jacket.

"Oh," I started, putting my hand protectively over the cover. "It's just my sketchbook."

"What were you working on?"

I knew he was asking to be polite and make conversation, but I never shared my sketches with anyone. Never even talked about them.

"Nothing ... just some dresses."

"So, like fashion design?" he asked, picking up his glass of water and looking at me with those sweet velvety eyes.

He still had the glasses on, and they were doing funny things to my insides.

"Yeah, I, uh, like to design clothes. Just fooling around," I said, hoping he'd take my answer and let it go.

"And do you actually make them? Like, sew them yourself and everything?" Noah asked, his tone sounding like he was sincerely curious.

"I can ... I mean, I have," I said, suddenly feeling anxious. "I've made a few things for myself, but it's mostly just something I do for fun ... for myself. I've never showed my pieces to anyone."

Noah blinked and looked down at the book I was still clinging to, before his eyes once again met mine.

"Not even Helen? Don't you both work in fashion?"

Okay, so he remembered her name. Not such a big deal, right? Except it felt like a big deal. It meant that Noah actually listened and retained the things we talked about. I think it took Jared months to remember Helen's name.

"We do, but, no ... not even Helen."

"Why not?"

I shrugged and said, "I don't know, I guess it feels too

personal, if that makes sense. If I show it to other people, then they're going to give their opinion, you know. And I'm not ready for that ... It's too personal to me, I guess."

"Sure, I understand that," Noah said with a nod. "I've had to publish articles and papers and am three quarters into a book. I know these things are important for my career and since I want to make tenure, I need to keep publishing, but some things are harder to share with the public than others. What you said about people needing to give their opinion, I agree with one-hundred percent. And I know they say that once you publish, the work is no longer your own, so you shouldn't take the reactions personally, but that's often easier said than done."

His words settled over me like a blanket. I loved that he understood where I was coming from. My insecurities.

I was so pleased that I was about to break my own rule and shove the book toward him, but before I could do so a young woman wearing a short skirt and halter top stopped next to our table.

I glanced up and saw her shoot me a glare before she turned toward Noah with a pout and arched her back slightly, so her breasts were more prominent.

"Mr. Mason," she said breathily, and I fought the urge to roll my eyes.

He looked up and momentary confusion crossed his features before the girl registered and he said, "Ms. Sinclair? What are you doing here?"

"I was grabbing something to eat and saw you, so thought I'd come over and say hi," she said, widening her eyes and leaving her lips slightly parted.

I glanced at Noah to gauge his reaction, and when he simply looked annoyed, I bit my lip to keep from smiling.

"Ms. Sinclair, my office hours begin at three. I'd appreciate it if you caught me there or after class."

She blinked and her shoulders seemed to sag.

"Okay, I guess, I'll see you then."

Noah nodded and turned his attention back to me.

Ms. Sinclair stood there for a few seconds, as if hoping he'd look up and realize what he was missing, but it was obvious in his mind their interaction was over.

When she walked away, I looked at him and asked, "Are all of your students in love with you?"

Noah's eyes widened and he looked honestly flabbergasted.

"What? No ... you sound like Trent. Ms. Sinclair is one of those students who's falling behind and needs help, that's all."

"You're adorable," I said sunnily, laughing lightly as his expression turned baffled.

"Thank you ... *I think*."

12

NOAH

"Suzy's going to be fine, Charles. I know she is," I assured my brother, even though I'd been in a cold sweat of fear ever since my mom had called me to tell me they'd taken Suzy to the emergency room.

She'd spiked a very high fever right before bed, and they hadn't been able to bring it down with infant Tylenol or a cool cloth. Charles had called our parents and my mom had suggested they bring her to the hospital.

Suzy was so little; it was better to be safe than sorry.

Of course, as soon as they'd hung up, our mom had called me and now we were all at the hospital together.

Jamilla was back with Suzy and Charles had come out to let us know the doctor was with them and they were administering antibiotics. My brother had looked so upset that I felt I needed to say something to try and help.

My parents were sitting next to each other, holding hands and drinking coffee, while I'd been staring at the small television without really registering what I was watching.

"Thanks, Noah. I'm gonna head back. You guys really don't have to stay. Suzy's gonna be fine," Charles said, but we all simply looked at him rather than protest.

There was no way any of us were leaving.

Once he was gone, I turned to my parents and asked, "Do you want anything from the vending machine?"

My mom shook her head, but my dad said, "Something salty."

"You got it," I replied, then left them to walk down the hall to where I'd seen the machines.

I was looking at my options when my phone gave a text alert.

It was Summer. I wasn't a fan of texting, it felt like a dispassionate way to communicate, but I'd been making an effort with her.

I suddenly felt the urge to hear her voice, so rather than fumble out a reply, I called her.

"Hey," she said warmly, sounding happy to hear from me, as she did every time I called.

It was really nice, comforting even, to have someone be delighted simply because I picked up the phone.

"Summer," I managed, embarrassed when my voice shook.

"Noah," she said, suddenly on alert. "Is everything okay?"

"I'm at the emergency room ... It's my niece. They say she's going to be fine, but she's so tiny ... I guess I'm more shook up over it than I realized."

"Oh no, I'm so sorry. But I'm happy to hear she's going to be okay. You said she's only around three months old?"

"She'll be four months on Tuesday."

"What hospital are you at?"

"General. She spiked a fever a few hours ago and they're working on bringing it down. When my mom called to tell me ... well, I've never felt that kind of fear before."

I probably shouldn't have called and there were probably rules about leaning on a woman you'd only recently started seeing about serious family issues, but hearing her voice was already making me feel better. Steadier.

"I'm sure. Are you there waiting by yourself?" Summer asked.

"No. My parents are here waiting with me and Charles and Jamilla are back with Suzy and the doctor."

"That's good. Please let me know if there's anything I can do."

"Just talking to you has helped, so thanks. Now I'm going to grab some snacks out of this vending machine and hopefully her temperature will be back to normal soon."

"Okay. I'll pray for her."

"Thanks, Summer. And thanks for listening."

I hung up feeling lighter than I had only moments before.

After selecting some chips for my dad and a Snickers bar for myself, I grabbed the items out of the bottom and headed back to where my parents were waiting.

Forty minutes later, all I had left was an empty Snickers wrapper and I was trying not to nod off in the uncomfortable chair I was sitting on. When Summer rounded the corner, I thought she was a vision at first.

A gorgeous, casual version of the woman I'd been seeing, with her blonde hair piled on top of her head and her body encased in some sort of silky track suit. Her face was free of makeup and looked scrubbed so clean it was shining, and in her hands, she carried a large box.

"Summer?" I asked, when I blinked and she was still standing in front of me, looking a little unsure of herself.

I quickly stood up and crossed to her. I couldn't believe she was there, but somewhere inside of me I felt grateful and relieved to see her. Like a weight had been lifted for some reason. Maybe it had to do with her sunny smiles and easy nature, but the effect of seeing her was calming.

"Hi," she said softly, her eyes darting to my parents and back again. "I wasn't sure if you would want me to come or not, but I thought you may be hungry and need some support, so I decided to just do it."

"I'm glad you did," I assured her with a small smile. "Let me take that for you."

"It's burgers and fries for everyone," she said as I took the box and placed it on the table by my parents. "Hi, I'm Summer."

My parents both stood, and I was pretty sure my mom winked at me, before moving to embrace Summer.

"Hello, Summer. It was so thoughtful of you to bring food for us. Thank you."

Summer's cheeks pinkened at my mother's praise. After my mother let her go, my father extended his hand to Summer.

"It's nice to meet you."

"Thank you, it's wonderful to meet both of you, Mr. and Mrs. Mason. I'm so sorry about your granddaughter."

"We appreciate that. Luckily, she's going to be just fine. Hopefully we'll be able to snuggle her soon. I know I won't feel better until I see and hold her myself."

I wrapped an arm around my mom's shoulders and hugged her briefly.

"Thanks, sweetheart. Now let's not let this food go to waste," she said, before looking up at me and whispering, "Your girl is lovely, Noah."

13

SUMMER

"Thanks so much for encouraging me to go to the hospital, Whit. It was the right decision," I told her when she joined Margo and me at our table. It was Thursday night, and we were settling in to enjoy some delicious southern barbecue. "Noah's family was so nice and seeing him really made me feel better."

After speaking to Noah the other night, I'd been conflicted over whether or not I should go be with him at the hospital. I wanted to, but things between us were so new I didn't know if he would want me there or if I would be overstepping.

I'd had an internal debate and finally called Whitney to get her opinion, which had been an emphatic "*Go*"!

Since that was what I'd wanted to hear anyway, I'd immediately grabbed my things and put in a to-go order at my favorite local burger place. When I'd walked into the waiting room and seen his face, I knew it was the right decision.

"Good, I told you you'd be welcome. When people are afraid and waiting in a hospital, it's always comforting to know someone cares. He'd have to be a fool not to want you there," Whitney said simply as she put her jacket over the back of the chair and sat down.

"I told her she should have followed him home and jumped him, given that extra bit of comfort," Margo said with a grin, then shrugged. "She didn't take *my* advice though."

I laughed and said, "Margo, we are nowhere near that stage in our relationship."

"Why the hell not?" she asked, sitting up in her seat and leaning forward. "How do you know you're compatible, that you have chemistry and passion, if you don't sample the goods? It would be horrible to start forming an emotional connection to Noah, only to find out he's like a dead fish in bed."

Whitney choked on her water as I shook my head.

"No, no way," I argued. "We kissed ... I felt sparks all the way to my toes and back. There's no way he's a fish, dead or otherwise."

"If you say so," Margo said, flopping back and taking a sip of her draft beer. "I've slept with guys who could kiss but had no idea how to please a woman in bed."

"God wouldn't be that cruel," I assured her. "Noah is sweet, funny, and so adorable I could cry. There's no way we won't be compatible once we get to that point."

"Yeah, Margo, don't be such a spoil sport. Summer really likes Noah."

"I'm not saying I hope he's a dead fish, I'm simply giving her a head's up that it could happen. I'm sure Noah will rock your world. He is a cutie. Sorry for disparaging his prowess."

Margo ran a hand over her long sleek hair and flipped it over her shoulder.

"That's okay, I know you're looking out for me," I said, giving her a sly glance. "I do have a way you could make it up to me, though."

"Oh, no," Margo replied. "I just walked right into that one, didn't I?"

Whitney gave a soft laugh. "I believe you did."

"What is it, sunshine?"

"Well, before I met Noah in person, I signed up for a speed

dating social with True Love. I can't cancel, because it would mess up their numbers and throw off the night for the other members, but, since I'm seeing Noah, even if we haven't made any promises or anything yet, I really wouldn't feel right attending."

"So?"

"So, you'd really be helping me out if you went in my place."

"Absolutely not," Margo said with a grimace. "You know I am not about that dating life."

"It's not really *dating*. You have some cocktails and sit in a booth and the guys rotate every five minutes. You don't really have to do anything at all, just sit there and meet a few new people. They're totally fun and stress free, I swear."

"Summer, you know I'd rather be dragged over hot coals than make small talk with a bunch of strange men looking for life partners."

"They're not," I said with a chuckle. "It's usually just guys who are looking to find a connection with someone. Just because they're on the app doesn't mean they're looking for a wife."

"Still sounds like a nightmare."

"Please?" I asked, giving her my best puppy dog look. "I'll owe you ... *big time*."

"Oh my gosh, don't give me those eyes. Fine, I'll do it. But trust and believe I will be calling in that favor. You won't know when, you won't know what, but it will happen."

"Jeez, that sounds ominous," I joked, before turning my full attention to Whitney and saying, "Now, fill us in on all the wedding prep."

"You know The Castle?" she asked.

I nodded emphatically. The Castle was a beautiful venue for events. Some rich guy had built a castle for his wife in the twenties. It was up on a hill with beautiful grounds that included a vineyard. After they'd passed, their children had sold it and it had been converted into a commercial space. Now people could rent it for a myriad of things, as long as they could afford it.

"You guys booked The Castle?" I cried, practically vibrating in my seat with excitement.

"We did. The owners have been clients of Luca's father for decades and they were able to fit us in in six weeks."

"Six weeks?" I gasped. "That's not enough time..."

"Mrs. Russo is a complete dynamo. You'd be surprised by how much she has set up and confirmed already. She's like my own personal wedding planner."

"Oh, well, that's great," I said, a little disappointed that Margo and I wouldn't be tapped to help out with the wedding. Sure, I knew Stella was Whitney's maid of honor, but since she was still a teenager, I'd been hoping we could get in there and be of some use.

"Actually, I was hoping you guys wouldn't mind helping out with the shower and bachelorette. I wasn't going to have either, but the Russos insisted. So, Stella wants to help plan the bridal shower, and Mrs. Russo is going to help her with that, but if you two wouldn't mind working with Charlotte on the bachelorette party, I would really appreciate it."

"We'd love to, right, Margo?" I asked her excitedly.

"Of course, we've got you, girl," Margo agreed, to which I clapped and said, "Yay!"

"Great, thanks. So really, everything is taken care of except for the dress. I've looked online and even allowed Luca's mom to drag me to a few dress shops, but I haven't found *the one* yet. I'm starting to wonder if it exists. I mean, I can't be the only woman in my forties who is on her second wedding and doesn't want something elaborate, right?"

I leaned down and put my hand in my purse, my fingers brushing against the spine of my sketchbook, and I tried to search for courage.

"Uh, I may have some ideas, actually," I forced myself to say, even though it came out barely above a whisper.

"You do?" Whitney asked.

When I didn't immediately answer, Margo prodded, "Well, show us. I wouldn't be surprised if you had a scrapbook of ideas."

"Not a scrapbook," I began, sitting back up and placing my book on the table.

"What's that?" Whitney asked gently, her eyes on my face as if she could see more than I wanted her to.

"It's my sketchbook."

"We didn't know you were an artist," Margo said, leaning on the table and getting closer, her expression full of interest.

"Not an artist exactly, but I do like to design and sketch clothes."

"That's amazing, Summer, why haven't you said anything?"

I gave a half shrug and said, "I've never actually shown any of my sketches to anyone. But I have made a few of the pieces for myself."

"Really? Anything we would have seen?"

I ran my finger over the cover and said, "That gray cutout dress I wore to your last house party."

"Wow, that dress looked fantastic on you," Whitney said. "You're obviously very talented. You shouldn't hide that from anyone."

"She's right. That dress was fire," Margo agreed.

I felt my eyes well as I took a deep breath and slowly pushed the book toward Whitney.

"The first ten sketches," I told her, then snatched my hand back before I lost my nerve and took the book back.

Whitney took the book almost reverently and opened it. Margo scooted her chair closer so she could look over her shoulder as Whit flipped the pages.

When she got to the last one, her breath caught, and her eyes flew to my face.

I knew she was looking at the floor-length fit and flare ivory lace with a champagne underlay. It had an exaggerated V, front and back, and as I'd drawn it, I'd known it would complement Whitney beautifully.

"Summer," she breathed, seemingly choked up with emotion. "This is gorgeous."

"It really is. You are extremely talented," Margo told me, and my heart swelled as their praise washed over me. Then she looked at Whitney and said, "And you would completely devastate Luca in that dress."

Whitney's smile turned almost wicked when she replied, "He wouldn't know what hit him," then she turned to me and said, "I have to have it."

14

NOAH

I looked around the room until my gaze landed on dishes from last night's dinner on the end table.

After glancing at my watch, I hurriedly rushed to pick it up and take it to the kitchen. Once there, I rinsed them and put them in the dishwasher. Which is when I got a load of all of the dishes stacked in the sink.

"Shoot!" I exclaimed as I started to put everything in the dishwasher, regardless of whether they'd been rinsed or not. *I'll fix it later*.

It's not like I was a slob, but no one would ever describe me as a neat freak either.

I'd lived alone for the past twelve years and had definitely fallen into some bad habits. But, when you worked all day and sometimes well into the night, and generally grabbed a quick meal alone while reading in the den, a spotless house was low on the list of priorities.

I did have a woman who came once a week to do deep cleaning, so all I really needed to do was maintain a level of cleanliness I was comfortable with.

Still, I doubted Summer would be impressed by a sink full of dishes, or last night's bourbon glass on the table.

I checked my watch again, letting out a sigh of relief when I saw I still had ten minutes until she was due to arrive.

Once the dishes were hidden away, I went into each room stacking papers and shelving books. I'd just finished shoving clothes from the chair in my bedroom into the hamper when the doorbell rang.

My stomach dipped in anticipation.

I never really had anyone over to my house, other than Trent and his family, and my own family, but when Summer had expressed an interest in spending a relaxing night in with takeout and a movie, I'd given her an impromptu invitation.

As I passed the decorative hallway mirror my sister-in-law had given me, I paused to give myself a quick inspection. After pushing the hair off my forehead and taking off my glasses and securing them in my shirt pocket, I deemed myself *as good as I was going to get* and moved to open the front door.

The sight of Summer standing on my porch, smiling sweetly at me, a large bag of terrific-smelling food in one hand, clad in form-fitting jeans and a simple green blouse, left me momentarily speechless.

"Noah," she prompted when I neither greeted her nor stepped aside to let her in.

"*Uh,* sorry, *yes, hi*. Please come in," I managed finally, moving to take the bag from her and let her inside.

I closed the door behind her and followed as she stepped into my house, her head swiveling to and fro as she seemed to take everything in at once.

"This place is great," Summer said as she crossed to one of the bookshelves in my living room and ran her hand over the shelf as she looked at the spines. "It's so sweet and welcoming from the outside."

"Thank you. My father always told me real estate was a good investment, and to never rent, so I actually bought this place about ten years ago."

"Wow. How many bedrooms is it?" she asked as she moved on to the next shelf.

"Three bedrooms, two baths, with an office and formal dining room," I replied, enjoying the way she seemed to brighten the space simply by being in it. "I can give you a quick tour before we eat if you'd like."

"Yeah, I would," Summer said, glancing at me from over her shoulder before moving on to the third and final shelf in the living room.

"Right this way," I said, and as we went from room to room, I tried to look at my home through her eyes.

Bookshelves in every room, including the dining room and breakfast nook, some practically overflowing with books. Neutral tones and the only accent pieces or art I owned were gifts, so there wasn't necessarily a theme so much as a hodge podge of items. Still, they somehow fit together.

One spare bedroom had a queen bed, the other a day bed, and neither had dressers or anything else in the room except bookshelves. No one had ever stayed over so long to necessitate anything other than a few hangers in the closet. The rooms were hardly ever opened, unless I was looking for a book.

My master and office, however, were fully outfitted and definitely looked lived in.

"I love this space," Summer said as we walked around my bedroom.

It was quite large, with a master bath, sitting area, and walk-in closet. The sitting area was a place I utilized almost daily, as I liked to grade papers in the recliner and often fell asleep reading there.

"Seeing your house makes me feel like I have a lot of growing up to do," Summer said, her tone light with laughter. "I've been renting an apartment since my divorce and if I'm being honest, it's a dump. I've been saving though, and I'd love to get myself a little house. It must feel great to know this is all yours."

"That's great," I told her as we moved down the hall toward

the kitchen where I'd left the food. "I do like having my own space and being able to make decisions on renovations and such, but it does suck when things break down and there's no one else to replace them but me."

Summer chuckled and started taking the takeout containers out of the bag and placing them on the counter.

"Mmm, it smells delicious," I exclaimed. I'd been nervous all day, hadn't eaten since breakfast, and was praying my stomach didn't growl out loud and embarrass me.

"I got the beef and broccoli for you, along with the fried rice. I also got us some spring rolls and crab Rangoon on the side, just in case."

"Perfect, I love it all," I said eagerly.

"Great," Summer said, beaming. "Did you pick a movie?"

"I have a couple options for you," I said, not wanting to put too much pressure on her, but curious what she would pick out of the choices I gave her.

"You know, I didn't see a TV on our tour."

I gave her what I hoped was a mysterious grin and said, "Don't worry, I've got us all taken care of."

15

SUMMER

He is so stinkin' cute!

We loaded our plates and took them back into the living room. Once there, Noah picked up a remote, pressed a button, and a large, curved screen TV rose out of the console against the wall.

It was the only surface not teaming with books, so I should have realized it was more than a cabinet.

"That's pretty cool," I said with a smile as we settled into his plush couch. "Are you sure you're okay with me eating on here?"

"Oh yeah, I do it all the time. I do have a small laptop table if you'd feel more comfortable with that."

"Sure, that would be great."

He placed his plate on the side table, then went to the closet and pulled out a small foldable table and placed it over my lap.

"Thank you," I said easily, resting my food on top of it and easing back, deep into the cushion.

"So," Noah began, his voice tinged with excitement. "Here are your movie choices ... *Pride & Prejudice*, the two thousand five version, *A Quiet Place*, or *Inception*."

"Those are very different," I replied, eyeing him curiously. "Why do I feel like this is a test."

He chuckled and shook his head, his expression sheepish and utterly adorable.

"No, not at all. These are simply three of my favorite movies and I'm curious which will appeal to you."

Still worried my answer *was* part of a test, even if he didn't realize it, I thought over the options. I'd actually already seen all the movies but wondered if *Pride & Prejudice* was too obvious a choice, or *Inception* too weird. *A Quiet Place* had given me nightmares, so I wasn't going to pick that one.

Deciding to simply be honest and choose the one I *wanted* to watch the most, I said, "*Pride & Prejudice*." Then asked in a rush, "Is that okay? Is that right?"

Noah smiled and said, "There's no right answer, and yes, *Pride & Prejudice* is perfect. It's a great retelling."

"Do you teach it as part of your curriculum?" I asked, curious to know more about him and his work.

"I have. This year I had them read and watch the most recent adaptation of *Little Women*. It felt more timely, since that movie is more current. I find the students can relate better and enjoy the assignment more if the adaptation is current."

"I bet they love it."

"I hope so," he said, going through the apps on his TV until he found the one he was looking for. "I think most of them do ... Of course, there are always outliers. People who take my class thinking it'll be an easy grade."

"I bet that's frustrating."

I picked up my chopsticks and fought with them until I had the correct hold, which usually took me a few tries, and then I took a small bite of my orange chicken. I didn't want to look like a pig at the trough and start mowing through my plate; instead, I would take small bites and be careful not to make a mess.

It was hard though because I was starving.

I looked up and over at Noah and I could swear he was trying to be just as delicate as I was.

"Is the food okay?" I asked.

"Yeah, it's great. I'm trying not to offend you by shoveling it into my mouth," he said with a wry laugh. "I forgot to eat lunch and I'm actually famished."

"Oh my gosh, me, too. And I was trying not to eat too fast," I admitted. "But what I really want to do is pick up this plate and pour it into my mouth."

We grinned at each other and when he said, "Let's not worry about being polite and simply eat how we normally would, all right? We'd have to eventually."

I felt warmth spread through me at his inadvertent suggestion that we'd be sharing more meals together and nodded in agreement.

"You're on."

Noah started the movie and we both finished our dinner.

After he'd cleared our plates and brought me a glass of wine, he showed me how to lift the recliner and we both settled in to enjoy the movie. When Mr. Darcy helped Elizabeth into her carriage, Noah reached for my hand and held it, causing my heart to skip a beat, and kept it in his through the rest of the movie.

Once the movie was over, we chatted about it briefly, before I caught his gaze with mine and said, "I wanted to thank you for your words the other day ... when we were discussing my sketches and you told me how it felt to you to publish your writing."

"I was simply being honest, there's no need to thank me."

"Well, because of that, I showed Whitney and Margo my sketches for her wedding dress."

"That's wonderful. I'm sure she was pleased."

"Very. Actually, she loved one of them and wants to wear it for her wedding."

I was smiling so hard my cheeks hurt. "I broke down and showed Helen as well, who chastised me for hiding my light under a bushel, and she is meeting with Whitney next week to take her measurements and start working on the dress. The wedding is in six weeks, so there's not a ton of time, but I know if anyone can make it happen, Helen can."

"Congratulations!"

"Noah, uh, I know we have only been seeing each other for a short while, and I don't want to sound presumptuous, *but* if we're still dating when the time comes, I'd love it if you would go to the wedding with me." I bit my lip and met his eyes. "I hope that doesn't freak you out."

He brought the hand he was *still holding* to his lips and kissed the back of my wrist.

"I would love to."

16

NOAH

I watched the joy spread over her face and felt pride in the fact that *I* had made her happy.

Summer was nothing like I'd expected when I'd first seen her in the bar. She'd seemed so unattainable and *way* out of my league. But being with her was fun, and easy, and I found myself looking forward to our every interaction.

I also found myself not wanting to let her go.

With a deep breath and a little mental pep talk, I opened my mouth to ask her something that was out of my comfort zone. I wasn't sure if she followed any of the *dating rules* some people seemed to abide by these days, or if she would think I was being too forward, but she'd taken a chance on asking me about the wedding, so I was going to take a chance as well.

"Summer, would you stay?" I said, losing my nerve halfway through and having to pause to breathe. "I mean, the night ... here with me."

Summer's lips turned up and she said, "I'd love that. Thank you for asking me."

"I want to be truthful with you and let you know this isn't a request I make often or take lightly. It's been a few years since I've made love with anyone. It's not that I don't enjoy sex, I do, but I've always needed a personal connection. I've never been one to hook up for the sake of doing so, not even in college. It just never appealed to me."

Once I'd gotten out everything, I took another cleansing breath and waited for her response.

"I'm the same way," Summer said, giving my hand a reassuring squeeze. "I haven't been with anyone since my ex-husband. And, honestly, he was only the second man I'd even been with, so I don't take this lightly either."

Her admission made me gulp. *I'd be the third man she'd ever been with*. I wasn't sure if that knowledge made me feel more, or less, pressure.

"So, it's been a while since you were in a serious relationship?" she asked, her tone curious.

I ran my free hand through my hair and admitted, "I guess I've never been in anything really serious. I had a girlfriend in high school, but I was a bit of a nerd. Always worried about keeping my GPA up so I could get into a good school. Plus, my dad was a professor, so I was always worried about letting him down."

"That's sweet. He seemed very nice."

"He's the best," I agreed with a grin. "And I must note, he didn't pressure me about my grades, it was all internalized. Anyway, then I was focused on doing well in college, and then work, so although I've dated, those relationships were never a priority." I winced as I heard my own words and said, "And that doesn't make me sound like a catch, does it?"

Summer gave a soft laugh.

"I think you're a man who knows what he wants and focuses on getting it. That's a good thing. *Great*, actually."

"Very astute," I said, enjoying how well she seemed to *get* me. *And still want to be around me, anyway*.

"How's your niece doing? Still feeling better, I hope."

"Yes, much. Thanks for asking. She really scared all of us for a minute there."

"It's sweet how enamored with her you are ... I could tell you all dote on her."

"Well, she's the first for all of us, so of course she's going to be a bit spoiled. It's the same with my friend Trent's son Tucker. He and Suzy were born weeks apart and they are really two of the most adorable, and brilliant, babies you've ever seen."

"I only saw her for a moment, but she was absolutely beautiful."

I nodded in agreement because it was the truth.

"It's so wonderful to be able to watch their development. Of course, I can't be there every day to see every little discovery, which is one of the reasons I can't wait to have kids, but I swear each time I see them, they've learned something new. It's amazing."

"I love that."

"Would you like another glass of wine?" I asked when I realized her glass was empty and probably had been for some time.

"Only if you're joining me."

I nodded and stood, grabbing both of our empty glasses and moving toward the kitchen.

I'd expected to be nervous to have Summer sleep over, but funnily enough, it felt right. Normal even, like having her in my home, talking and drinking wine, was a regular occurrence.

It was nice. Comfortable. Right.

When I joined her back in the living room, two full glasses in hand, I asked, "Shall we adjourn to the sitting area in my room?"

Her eyes widened momentarily, before she stood up slowly, deliberately, and a downright seductive look came over her.

The first stirrings of nerves hit deep in my belly.

Good Lord, she is gorgeous.

"Sounds perfect," Summer said, crossing to take her glass from me, before walking past me and leading *me* to *my* room.

When she glanced at me over her shoulder, I was sunk. It was like my mind was no longer driving this train, and I could barely string together two words as my body reacted to everything she was putting out.

"Music?" I managed to spit out inelegantly as I pushed aside some papers to put my glass down.

"Music sounds lovely," she said, and I swear her voice sounded like a purr. One I felt vibrate right through me.

I opened the lid to my record player and pulled out a record from the stack, turning toward Summer, my mouth open ready to speak. But when I saw her perched on the edge of my bed, no sound came out.

Summer gave me a knowing smile and patted the bed next to her in invitation.

"Jazz?" I asked and was mortified when it came out as a squeak.

17
SUMMER

I wasn't always the most outgoing person in the bedroom. In fact, Jared had often accused me of not being aggressive enough, but being with Noah felt different.

He made me feel sexy and desirable, which gave me confidence and had me wondering what he would be like when he wasn't being so polite. So poised and in control.

The look on his face when he'd turned and seen me sitting on the edge of his bed had me feeling like I could take on the world, and I was planning to start in his bedroom. I found I was enjoying the sense of power; it was almost like I was a vixen.

Or Margo.

Noah fumbled around with the record player, and once the smooth jazz sounds filled the room, he started slowly toward the bed.

I moved my hand so he could sit where I'd indicated and when he did, I stood and placed myself in front of him. When his eyes were on me, I placed my hands on the hem of my shirt and pulled it over my head, letting it drop to the floor next to me.

His gaze immediately dropped to my breasts, which had me preening in delight.

I loved my breasts. They were magnificent. Large, full, and perfectly rounded with sensitive rose-colored nipples, which were already straining against the lace fabric of my Fleur du Mal balconette bra.

I didn't know if Noah would ask me to stay, or if things would progress past the heavy petting and kissing stage, but I'd wanted to be prepared just in case. I'd put on my best lingerie and now I was so glad I had, because Noah's eyes were transfixed, and his mouth had gone slightly slack as he took in my soft flesh spilling over the delicate cups.

Loving his gaze on me, I peeled off my jeans and kicked them to the side, exposing the matching lavender lace thong. Then I placed my palms on my thighs and began to move them up.

Noah's eyes lowered and began tracking my movements. Up over my hips, pausing briefly, before crossing plains of my stomach to reach the underside of my breasts. I cupped them briefly, caressing the lace with my thumbs before moving to the straps.

"No," Noah choked out, seeming to come out of a trance when he realized I was about to take off the bra. "Please, let me."

He stood abruptly, which brought him so close our thighs touched, so I took a step back to give him room to move.

I bit my lip as he raised his hand to touch, anticipation making my body heat before we'd even made contact. His knuckles against my stomach made me gasp, and when he reached around to unhook my bra, I could feel his hands quivering.

It was the sweetest thing.

The straps fell slowly from my shoulders and down my arms and Noah caught the lace before it could fall, turning to lay it reverently on the bed behind him, before turning back and taking in my naked breasts.

"You're gorgeous," he breathed, his tongue darting out to wet his lips as his eyes darkened.

"Touch me," I begged, not caring if I sounded needy, because

I so totally was. Feeling his hands on my skin seemed like the greatest gift I could ever receive, and I was moments away from it happening.

A low sound, almost like a growl, emitted from his lips as Noah touched me for the first time.

It felt wonderful. Erotic and sweet at the same time, and I let my head fall back as he simultaneously pinched one nipple and bent to put the other in his mouth.

"Yes," I whispered, bringing a hand up and into his hair, reveling in the softness of it as he teased my body.

He caressed and licked and nibbled softly, his mouth on a delicious exploration that I could only enjoy. When the tugs on my nipples struck me straight down to my core, I began to feel itchy with the need for more.

With my free hand, I reached between us until I could grasp one of his, then I urged it down to the scrap of material currently providing a barrier between my legs. Once I placed it where I wanted it, I surged my hips forward, letting him feel the wet heat waiting there, begging for attention, before doing my best to rid myself of the lace, freeing myself for his discovery.

Noah did not disappoint. His fingers ran gently over my folds, and I widened my stance to give him greater access.

The little grunts and groans he let out made me almost as crazy as the fingers he'd dipped into my body.

"Ride them, Summer," he demanded, causing my eyes to fly open with shock at the commanding tone.

Oh my God, I thought, doing as he asked as I watched determination cross his face. He was unbelievably sexy as he worked so studiously at bringing me pleasure. I moved my hips as he thrust his fingers in and out and then moved his thumb to the bundle of nerves at my center, dying for his attention.

My breath started coming out in little pants as the pleasure grew.

"Noah," I moaned, then I lost his eyes as he bent to bite

down on my nipple as his thumb brought me to a screaming release.

I came down slowly, smiling with satisfaction as he gathered me into his arms and held me close.

"That was amazing," I said when my breathing had evened out enough to speak.

Noah shifted back so he could kiss me softly.

"It was," he agreed.

"Now, I need you inside of me," I told him matter of factly." But first, I need you out of these clothes."

"Are you sure?" he asked, brushing his lips across mine once more.

"I have never been more sure of anything in my life."

18

NOAH

"Congratulations, Professor, on making tenure and your promotion to associate professor. There will be a ceremony and celebratory dinner, of course. I will send those details out shortly."

"Thank you, ma'am," I said, before shaking her hand and leaving her office in a daze.

I can't believe it; I've actually made it.

I'd known it was a possibility, of course, since I was the one who'd put in the application, but I was still delighted by the outcome.

I moved quickly through the halls and out of the building so I could get to the English building before my next class. I had some time, but I liked to get there early and have all of my preparations out and ready for the start of class.

When I reached the steps to the building, I may have been so thrilled I almost skipped up them, which normally I would never do, since it was undignified, especially of an *associate professor*. But my excitement level had reached epic proportions.

When I reached for the door handle, the door swung open before I made contact and I glanced up to see Trent grinning at me.

"You got it," he stated.

"I did," I replied happily. "How did you know?"

"Your Fred Astaire number up the stairs," he quipped.

I felt my cheeks heat but shook it off.

"*Associate professor with tenure*," I said, even though he already knew. It simply felt good to say it out loud.

"Congratulations, brother, you deserve it," Trent said, giving me a clap on the back.

"Thanks. You're next," I told him as I fell into step beside him.

"We shall see," he replied, but I knew he was downplaying things. He'd be up to apply next year, and I knew he'd get it. Not only did he work hard, but he had a family to think of, and I knew he always put their welfare and security first. "You'll have to let me know when the party is. I know Cam would kill for a night out, especially if it's to celebrate you."

"I will," I assured him, pausing before the door to my lecture hall. "Drinks tonight?"

"You bet."

The rest of the day went smoothly. I was in such a great mood that nothing was going to bring me down, not even my students and their oftentimes strange goings on.

"Mr. Mason, can you read that last passage again? I didn't quite get it and I feel like everything sounds better when you read it," Ms. Sinclair asked.

"Jesus, Natalie, give it a rest," Ms. Jordan, one of my brightest students, muttered. "You're embarrassing yourself."

"Ladies," I warned, not wanting them to start bickering, which is what often happened when the two of them had outbursts in class. "Yes, Ms. Sinclair, I can read it again, but it was the assigned reading over the weekend, so if you didn't understand it, you should have mentioned it at the beginning of class when I asked if anyone had issues with the material."

Ms. Sinclair gave a little huff and Ms. Jordan smirked, but I ignored them and continued on with class.

Once I was in my office, I took the time to call my parents, and then Summer, to let them know the good news.

My parents were thrilled, although they both said they knew it would happen. And Summer had squealed with delight. So loud that I'd had to hold the phone away from my ear for fear of a rupture.

"I'm so proud of you!" she cried. "I remember you saying you were working toward tenure, but I didn't realize you were already up for promotion. That's wonderful. I'll have to have you over this weekend for dinner. I'll make you my specialty."

"I can't wait," I replied, interested in seeing her apartment and trying out her *specialty*. "I'll call you later to set up the time."

"Okay. Congrats again."

I'd hung up with a smile, which remained on my face well past office hours and all the way to the bar.

"There he is," Trent called as I joined him at our usual spot. "A man who's got everything going for him ... a great job, a beautiful new girlfriend, and the best friend a man could have."

"There's that modesty again," I joked as I got up on the stool.

"I try. And I noticed you didn't contradict my girlfriend moniker."

"It is true that things between Summer and I have progressed, and I feel comfortable with her having that title," I told him as I reached for the draft the bartender set in front of me.

"I love it when you talk all formal..."

I shook my head, ignoring him. Trent loved to rib. He often said he wanted his funeral to be a roast rather than a solemn affair.

"Summer's amazing," I said, less formally. "I really enjoy spending time with her."

"Did you tell her about the promotion?"

"I did."

"And will she be joining us at the celebration dinner?" he asked, holding his phone in his hand.

"I haven't asked her yet, but I will, and I'm sure she'll say yes."

He started typing on his phone at my reply.

"What are you doing?"

"Cam wanted to know if Summer would be there, so I'm letting her know. She's dying to meet her. Says she has to meet the woman who makes the sexy professor tongue-tied."

"No one calls me that. And Summer doesn't make me tongue-tied."

"Uh, yeah, she does ... I'm pretty sure you almost swallowed your tongue when her friend Margo came over. And not only do your students call you the sexy professor, but Cam and I call you it all the time."

"Why?" I asked, honestly baffled.

"Because it gets you flustered, which is totally hilarious," he said, sounding as if I were obtuse.

"But why would it be hilarious if I'm not there to get flustered?"

"Because I can imagine your face in my head." He shrugged. "Plus, it's just a thing Cam and I do. It's our nickname for you."

"Well, I don't like it," I grumbled.

"I know," Trent said with an annoying chortle.

"Sycophant."

"Sexy professor."

Ugh.

19

SUMMER

"Are you excited about your bridal shower next weekend?" I asked Whitney, wriggling in my seat with enough excitement for all of us.

"Sure, I think it will be nice for all of us to get together, but Luca and I don't really need anything. We have already combined two households, which left us with more than we can manage," Whitney said, lifting her long brown hair off her neck as she pulled it up into a bun. "I tried to explain that to his mom and tell her I don't need to have the shower, but she insisted and said everyone is looking forward to it."

"I know I am," I gushed, reaching out to place my hand over hers on the table. "And don't worry, you won't end up with five blenders and a million dish towels. Promise."

Whitney looked over at me, her eyes full of suspicion.

"Why? What do you know?"

I pretended to lock my lips together and throw away the key, so she turned toward Margo.

"I'm staying out of it," was our friend's reply.

She was currently moving her potatoes around her plate aimlessly, which was unlike her. Margo ate like she did everything else in life, with gusto.

"Everything okay?" Whitney asked.

"Yeah, are you all right?" I added, concerned.

Margo looked up at us and sighed. "I slept with Carson the other night."

"Your ex-husband, Carson?" Whitney prodded.

My first instinct was to shout, "*Why?*", but I didn't want to upset Margo or make her think I was judging her, so I slid closer to her on the booth and put my arm around her shoulders.

"What happened?" I asked.

Margo sighed and dropped her fork, letting it clatter across her plate, before picking up her wine and taking a sip.

"Carson and I were coworkers before we were anything else. Eventually we worked so closely together we became good friends. Everyone at the office always joked around and called me his work wife, which I found extremely frustrating. I mean, seriously, just because a man and a woman work closely together, there has to be a label put on it. I found it demeaning. He and I were on the same level and calling me his *wife* seemed to indicate I was somehow less of an asset to the company than he was, like I had to defer to him. Honestly, it pissed me off."

"I bet," Whitney said, which made Margo throw up her hand and say, "Right?"

"Anyway, as the years went on, our friendship changed, and we started to hook up occasionally. We essentially worked all the time, so there wasn't much time to go out and meet people, and we both had needs to be met, so we started a mutually beneficial relationship."

Margo had never opened up to Whitney and me and shared her story, so when she paused, I asked eagerly, "And then what happened?" because I was dying to find out.

"It's such a cliché, but we were on a business trip in Vegas and after a night of drinking and gambling, we got married. Oh, the guys at work had a field day over that one. Now I wasn't only Carson's work wife, but his actual wife. When we got home, I wanted to get an annulment, but Carson talked me into give us a shot, so we did."

"How long did it last?" Whit asked.

Margo scoffed and said, "Until I got promoted above him. He couldn't handle it, me making more money and having a higher position in the company. He started sleeping around. I divorced his ass as soon as I found out, but old habits die hard, and since the divorce we've had the occasional hookup."

"Okay," I said, understanding even though I thought Carson deserved to have his balls set on fire. "So, what was different about this time? Why are you upset about it? Did something happen?"

Margo collapsed back against the booth and laid her head back.

"He's getting married. He told me as he was putting his pants back on."

"What an asshat," Whitney said in angry hushed tones. "Why didn't he say something before you slept together?"

"Because he knew I wouldn't sleep with him if I knew. I've always been vocal about my no cheating policy."

"*Dick*," I breathed.

"Yeah, he is," Margo agreed. "It's not like I want him for myself or regret divorcing him. I slept with him because we had good chemistry. But for him to do me like that, well, it made me lose what little respect for him I had left."

"I'm so sorry, Margo."

"Yeah," I agreed. "I hate that he hurt you again."

Margo sat up suddenly and shook her head.

"Okay, enough of that shit. Pity party over. Let's get another round of drinks and talk about something more pleasant. Like ... Summer, have you and that adorably clueless professor had sex yet, or what?"

I felt my cheeks warm, but I couldn't stop myself from practically shouting, "Yes!"

"Finally," Margo said, as she signaled to the waiter another round. "*I* was getting blue balls waiting for you two to finally take the plunge."

"Yay," Whitney cheered. "Tell us everything."

"Yeah, don't leave anything out."

Giddy with excitement over Noah, I happily shared my experience with Noah, although I kept some of the more intimate details to myself. By the time we were done, Margo was looking more like herself and even got the waiter's number before she left.

20

NOAH

As I pulled into the apartment complex, I had to double check the address to make sure I'd put it in the GPS correctly.

The place was run down, which Summer had mentioned, and the area of town wasn't the best.

I parked in the guest parking spot, just as she'd told me, and grabbed the cake I'd bought from the passenger seat before I got out of my car and followed her instructions to take the stairs and turn left to her apartment.

Once I got to the correct number, I shifted the cake to one hand and knocked, my head swiveling as I checked out my surroundings.

Seconds later, the door opened, and Summer was standing before me, beaming up at me in leggings and an oversized sweatshirt.

"Hey, come on in," she said happily, stepping to the side to let me in.

I surveyed the room as she shut the door behind me and thought, *Okay, this makes much more sense*.

The living space was bright and cheerful, with lots of yellows, pinks, and baby blues. The walls were adorned with canvas paintings. There were silhouettes of women walking the streets of Paris, Rome, and London, as well as prints of daisies, sunflowers, and seascapes.

There was a lot going on, but for some reason, it all worked beautifully. *It is quintessentially Summer*.

"I brought a lemon cake," I told her, lifting the box in my arms as evidence.

"Oh, yum, you can set it on the counter," she said, gesturing toward the kitchen, which was right off the living room. It was an open concept, with a long counter separating the two rooms.

There were two doors, other than the entrance, one off the living room, and one off the kitchen. Since Summer told me it was a one-bedroom apartment, I figured one of the doors led to her room and the other was some sort of closet or pantry.

"It smells great in here," I said, breathing in scents of garlic, oregano, and something else I couldn't quite place. "What are you making?"

"It's my meatloaf, along with mashed potatoes and some roasted brussels sprouts," Summer said, her tone somewhat shy.

"Wow, really? That sounds fantastic."

"Why don't you have a seat while I finish up," she suggested, pointing to one of the stools on the side of the counter.

I put down the cake box and took a seat, just as Summer got a beer out of the fridge, opened it, and placed in in front of me.

"Thanks," I said, taking a sip. "So, what makes this your specialty?"

"It's one of the only things my mom taught me to make. At least, the basic recipe. Over the years I've tweaked it and added ingredients until I got it the way I liked it. And now she usually asks me to make it for her every few months. It makes a few portions, so she can have leftovers, which she likes."

"So, you still see her a lot?"

"Probably not as much as I should, but I get over there when I can. I hate to say it, but I usually end up leaving sad or feeling bad about myself, so it always feels like a real chore to go."

I frowned, hating that for her. Summer deserved a family who cherished her and celebrated the wonderful person she was, not someone who made her feel like crap. I wished she could have had parents like my own.

"I'm sorry," I said, feeling like it was a lame but true sentiment.

"That's okay," Summer said with an easy shrug. She picked up her own beer and held it out, so I complied and lifted mine as well. She tapped the necks together and said, "Cheers."

"Cheers."

"So, I bet you were thrilled to find out about your promotion, huh? I'm so happy for you, and I'm glad you're willing to celebrate such an accomplishment with me."

"Of course," I said, my stomach growling as she started to plate up the food. "Actually, I wanted to ask you if you'd like to come with me to the faculty dinner to celebrate all of the promotees."

Summer paused with a spoon full of mashed potatoes hanging above the plate.

"You want me to come to a work function with you?"

"Yes."

"Like a 'get dressed up and mingle with your coworkers' kind of deal?"

"Exactly," I said, wondering why her eyes were getting bigger.

Summer squealed, startling me so I almost dropped my beer.

"I'd love to," she said, dropping the spoon on the plate and dancing around the counter to throw her arms around me.

"Trent and his wife, Cam, will be there. Maybe my parents. Those are the important people, everyone else will just be staff."

"Oh, I can't wait. I'm sure Cam and I will get along fabulously."

I grinned at her and agreed. "I know you will."

"When is it?" she asked, her arms still resting casually around my neck, as if we held each other all the time.

I found I really liked it.

"It's looking like next Friday night, but I'll let you know once it's confirmed."

"That's perfect. I'll have your dinner on Friday and Whitney's bridal shower on Saturday. It's going to be such a fun weekend."

"Actually, our faculty dinners are kind of boring," I warned her.

"I promise you won't be bored with me there," she said with a saucy wink.

I chuckled and replied, "I believe you."

21

SUMMER

"Hey, Mom," I called out as I opened the door to her house.

I made sure to shut and lock the steel security door before closing and locking the front door.

My mom's neighborhood had steadily been getting worse over the years, and although there hadn't been any thefts or crime, she was paranoid about someone breaking in. She made sure all the windows and doors were locked at all times, even though everything was reinforced with steel bars.

"Back here," she called, her voice coming out weak and raspy.

She'd been a pack-a-day smoker for as long as I could remember, and as far as she was concerned, that was never going to change.

I looked around the unkept space as I moved through the living room to her bedroom. There were dirty dishes and random trash scattered about, along with a couple overflowing ashtrays.

With a sigh, I shook my head and continued down the hall.

"How are you feeling?" I asked as I entered her room.

She was laying on the bed, a lit cigarette dangling from her mouth, her eyes glued to the small old TV sitting atop her dresser.

It looked like she was watching a soap opera.

"I didn't think they still made those," I remarked as I stepped closer.

"There are only a few left, but *General Hospital* has always been my favorite anyway, so that's all I care about."

"I brought you some leftovers. I made meatloaf the other night and thought you might like some. You can have it for lunch."

"Just set it down over there," she said, gesturing her cigarette toward an empty spot on the bed next to her. There wasn't must space left, since the surface was covered with old magazines, a paperback, and a bunch of used paper plates.

"Can I get you anything? A drink?" I asked, itching to go back into the other room and start cleaning.

"Coke if I have any," was her reply.

I found an almost empty two-liter in the fridge and poured it into a glass to take to her. Once I'd placed it on her nightstand, I quickly left her to her show and rolled up my sleeves as I mentally thought out the most efficient way to tackle the job ahead.

First, I walked to the kitchenette to grab one of the gallons of vinegar I left under the sink and poured some in a pot to boil on the stove. Then I walked around and refilled the small bowls I kept around the house.

Vinegar was one of the few things that would help get the smell of cigarette smoke out of her house. I also had some of those automatic spray air fresheners strategically placed around, but without the vinegar to take away the smell, the air freshener would just partially mask it, which just made the house smell like smokey violets.

Once that was done, I put the vinegar away and got out a large trash bag. I started in the living room, then moved to the kitchen, bathroom, and finally, the bedroom. My mother always complained when I was picking up in her space, so I usually tried to save it for last and get in and out as quickly as possible.

"Dammit, Summer, do you have to be doing that during my shows? Can't a woman get some *goddamn peace* in her own home?"

"Sorry, I'll just be a minute," I muttered, grabbing trash and shoving it in the bag.

I left the full bag by the front door to take out when I left and moved back to the kitchen to get the Windex and a rag. I cleaned as much as I could, then grabbed the vacuum. I'd have to skip vacuuming her room, since she was in there watching her shows. If she was in the kitchen, or even sitting on the ratty old couch, she could usually tolerate the noise, but not when she'd confined herself to a day in bed, which I knew was the case today.

After everything was as clean as it could get, I put all the supplies back where I got them and turned off the burner before going back to see my mother.

"Can I get anything else for you before I go?"

She looked at me for the first time since I'd arrived and scowled.

"Leaving so soon? So, you think all you gotta do is bring me your old food and disrupt my shows and then you've fulfilled your obligation as a daughter? No time to actually sit down and visit?"

"You usually don't want me to talk to you when you're watching your shows," I said calmly, not wanting to get into a fight with her.

"Since when do you care about what I want? With your high-falutin self ... fancy cars and rich old guys who do nothing but treat you like trash. Guess your shit stinks just like the rest of us."

"Mom," I whispered, hoping she'd stop.

"I told you that Jared would step out on you just like he did his other wife, but you didn't believe me. Thought your magic vagina would make him stay, but I told you so. Now he's filled up some new hussy's belly with the baby you always wanted. Bet that stings, doesn't it."

My throat started to burn, and my nose stung, but I tried to shake it off.

If my mother saw any sort of reaction, she'd only get worse.

"I've got to go to work, so I'm going to get going. You call if you need anything, okay?" I was proud when my voice came out strong and not shaky.

She scoffed.

"Yeah, get your fancy ass down to Helen and her fancy shop with her clothes no one in their right mind would shop at." Her lips got thin, and her eyes hardened. "Two-hundred dollars for a shirt ... ridiculous."

"Don't say that. Helen's your best friend. She's been there for you since you were little," I said, hoping to get through, but when she shifted, I noticed the top of a liquor bottle peaking up from beneath the blanket.

I should have known she'd been drinking.

"Yeah, some best friend, living up on her high horse while I rot away in this shithole."

Knowing nothing good would come out of staying in this situation, I told her once more I was leaving and then got out of there as fast as my heels would take me.

22

NOAH

I fiddled with my bow tie as I waited for Summer to finish getting ready.

It was Friday evening, and we were heading to the faculty dinner celebrating the new promotes. I'd been excited about it until I saw the attire was formal and realized I'd have to wear a tie.

Why anyone thought it was a good idea to voluntarily wear a noose around their neck, I had no idea.

It was the worst invention ever.

"Stop messing with it, it looks great."

I turned toward the sound of Summer's voice and was struck dumb by the sight of her. Her dress was black and form fitting, showing off her generous curves to perfection. The straps were off the shoulder and there was a long slit up her left thigh.

Her eyes were knowing, and her grin could only be described as mischievous as she spun around in front of me to show me that the dip in the back mirrored the front.

"Holy Toledo!" I exclaimed.

Summer giggled and said, "I'd hoped you'd like it."

"Like it? It's honestly the best thing I've ever seen, including the first time I saw Suzy, but if you tell my family I said that I'll deny it with my dying breath."

"My lips are sealed."

We closed up Summer's place and walked out to my car. It was a nice night so far, not too cool, so she'd decided to forgo any kind of jacket. I had to admit, I was one-hundred percent on board with her decision not to cover up the dress.

As I pulled out of the lot, Summer turned to me and asked, "What does that mean, anyway? Holy Toledo. I've always wondered."

"Oh, well, there are a few different meanings, actually. Toledo, Spain was the first city in the region to embrace Christianity. Then there's the more recent in Toledo, Ohio, nineteen twenties and thirties, to be exact. It was agreed upon between the police and the gangsters of the time, that if the cops would leave them alone, they would leave Toledo alone. So, it became a sanctuary. And finally, there's a sexual meaning..."

Once I recalled the meaning my cheeks reddened and I started stumbling over my words.

"Trent, uh, actually told me about that one. But it's not something I feel comfortable repeating."

"Really?" Summer said, laughing lightly. "Must be a doozy."

I tugged at my bow tie again. It suddenly felt extremely hard to breathe.

"Mm," I muttered noncommittally.

Summer leaned back in her seat and let out a happy sigh, and I knew she was letting me off the hook.

Is it any wonder I'm falling for her?

Wait. *What?*

If I hadn't been driving, I would have slid right out of my seat. Instead, I sat up taller, trying to look cool and not like I'd just completely freaked myself out.

"Is everything okay?" Summer asked softly from beside me.

I shot her a quick glance before turning my eyes back toward the road. "Uh, yeah, why?"

"You look like someone just shoved a rod in your spine all of a sudden."

"Oh, look, we're here," I muttered as I swung into the parking lot.

Once I found a spot, I parked and hurried around the car to open Summer's door.

"Thank you," she said, her hand in mine causing a jolt to run up my arm. She got out of the car and tucked her arm through mine.

The restaurant was one the admin of the school seemed to love, since they chose it for every function we had. I didn't mind. I enjoyed the ambience, which was kind of leather and stuffy, like an old cigar bar but without the smoking.

And they served the best crab cakes I'd ever had.

I walked in with my head held high, proud to have Summer on my arm, but inside I was a mass of confusion.

Summer and I hadn't known each other *that* long in the grand scheme of things, so there was no way I could *actually* be falling for her, right? It defied the laws of, well, my life. I'd never been one to jump into things, but rather the guy who eased into the shallow end until each section of my body was comfortable with being submerged.

"If it isn't the man of the hour," Trent said as he and Cam met us in the banquet room.

"*Water*," I said, strangely and without prompting.

"What?" he asked.

"What? I mimicked, unsure of what I said.

"Did you say you want water?"

"Uh, yeah," I replied, suddenly thinking a glass of water sounded magnificent.

Trent gave me a curious look, but simply said, "They have water at the tables. Do you want to get a drink at the bar, too?"

"That sounds good."

"Sorry for these two and their rudeness," Cam said, grabbing my attention. "I'm Cam, this one's better half."

Oh crap.

"I'm so sorry," I said hurriedly. "Summer, this is Cam and Trent, who you've seen before, and guys, this is Summer."

I really need to pull myself together.

They all shook hands and I glanced at Summer and asked, "What would you like to drink?"

"White wine," she said easily, completely unruffled by my behavior.

I nodded and indicated for Trent to lead the way.

"Everything okay, man?" Trent asked when we got to the bar and out of earshot.

I did some sort of laugh, head shake combo, that had him narrowing his eyes on me.

"Spill," he said.

"I think I'm falling in love with Summer," I whispered.

"No shit. Well, who could blame you? Have you seen that dress?" Trent looked over his shoulder at Summer and I had the sudden urge to punch him. "I mean, even Cam is falling in love over there. It's totally understandable. She's a terrific woman."

I followed his gaze to see Summer laughing at something Cam said and was struck anew by how she made me feel.

"She really is," I said with a sigh. "But I've never felt this way. I never expected it to happen so fast. What if it's just infatuation? I don't want to speak too soon and then be wrong."

"Then wait. Wait until you're sure of your feelings. And once you know you love her, shout it from the rooftops. You deserve happiness, but you don't have to say anything until you're comfortable with your feelings and feel confident in sharing them."

"Thanks," I said as I grabbed our drinks. "That's actually good advice."

"I know, right? It doesn't happen often, but when it does ... gold."

The ladies had found our table and joined my parents. I placed our drinks on the table and bent to give Summer a quick kiss and reassuring smile before taking my seat beside her. She shot me a wink before turning to Trent on her other side.

"Hey," I heard her whisper. "What does *Holy Toledo* mean?"

Trent let out a bark of laughter and I covered my face with my hands.

Lord, save me.

23

SUMMER

"Everything looks so beautiful," I gushed as I walked around the party room in the Italian restaurant Whitney's bridal shower was being held in.

I guess Luca's mom had wanted to have it at her house and cook everything, but everyone had talked her out of it, saying this way she could simply enjoy being mother of the groom and not be working the whole time.

From the look on her face as she tried the hors d'oeuvres on the table, she was not impressed.

The room had been decorated in Whitney's wedding colors, which were going to be dusty blue and gold with lots of greenery. And if this room was any indication, her actual wedding was going to be positively gorgeous.

The tablecloths were dusty blue with gold accents on the table and there were fresh green plants located all around, giving it an elegant and earthy feel.

Stella and Mrs. Russo had really outdone themselves.

"I'm not gonna lie, I dig it," Margo agreed, holding out her glass of champagne and tapping it against mine. "Cheers. To Whit and Luca."

"To Whit and Luca," I agreed, unable to keep from smiling, I was so excited for them. "She's going to be thrilled when she finds out about the gifts."

Since they knew Whitney and Luca didn't need the usual shower gifts, and they'd already requested no wedding gifts, Stella and Mrs. Russo had asked all of the guests to give honeymoon-related gifts.

Lingerie, gift cards to places in Fiji, which is where they were honeymooning, money ... things like that. That way, everything would be functional, and their honeymoon would be basically paid for.

"What did you get her?" I asked Margo.

"The dirtiest lingerie I could find," she replied with a smirk. "What about you?"

"The prettiest lingerie *I* could find."

Margo laughed and said, "Sounds about right. So, how was the dinner last night? Did you get along with his friends and family?"

"Yeah, they're all really great. And it was cute how nervous he got when they called his name and he had to go up and speak. I mean, he's a teacher, I'd think he'd be comfortable in front of a crowd."

"It's different when it's for something personal."

"I get that," I said, then leaned in and said softly, "He did seem a little off though. When he picked me up everything was fine, but something happened in the car on the way there, he got all stiff or something and never really shook it off."

"Hmmm, was it something you were discussing?"

I shook my head, still baffled by it all.

"No, well, maybe. He was telling me the meaning of the phrase, *Holy Toledo*. After he told me the two historical facts, he said there was another, sexual meaning, but he couldn't say it. I let it go at that, but afterwards *is* when he got weird. Do you think that was it?"

"I don't see why, unless it was an act he's performed himself."

My eyes widened as I looked at her. *No, that couldn't be it, could it?* I watched Margo's lips turn up and then wondered, *Has she done it?*

She must have read my look because she laughed and said, "No, I haven't done it."

"*Whew*," I said with relief. "That would have been TMI."

"She's here," someone called out and we all turned to watch as Whitney entered the room.

She looked surprised and delighted as she took it all in. "Thank you all so much for coming."

Whitney walked around and started greeting all her guests and I saw Helen enter and wave to get my attention.

She was carrying a garment bag, which I knew contained Whit's wedding dress. I'd seen it a few times during the process of being made, but I'd yet to see the final product. I'd wanted to wait and see it for the first time on Whitney with everyone else.

Whit had invited Helen to bring it to the shower and she was going to try it on and do a big reveal for everyone in attendance. It wasn't the traditional way of doing things, but Whitney was excited to see it on and wanted to share it with all her friends and family.

Instead of being all together at a bridal shop, we'd be seeing it at the shower.

Fun!

"Oh, you're here!" I exclaimed as I met up with Helen. "I'm so excited to see it I can barely stand it."

"It's gorgeous, Summer. You have a real talent," Helen said, looking at me with pride. "I'd love to go over more of your sketches and talk about doing some pieces for the store."

I was so full of love and joy at her words, I wouldn't be surprised if I was literally glowing.

We enjoyed the hors d'oeuvres, dessert bar, and unlimited champagne. Before presents, Whitney disappeared into the back with Helen to put on the dress and I waited with barely contained excitement.

"I can't stand it," I told Margo.

"It's going to be perfect," she assured me.

When Whitney walked back into the room, it went dead quiet, except for the sound of Mrs. Russo's delighted gasp.

My eyes filled as I watched her turn slowly for the crowd.

"It's the most amazing..." I lost my words as the tears spilled over onto my cheeks.

Suddenly, everyone started talking at once. Whitney held up her hand to quiet them and said, "Thank you, but this beautiful gown would not be possible without one of my best friends, Summer. She's the designer and *I think* she totally hit the nail on the head."

"To Summer," Margo said, raising her glass.

The ladies in the room echoed her sentiment and I knew it was a moment I would cherish forever.

24

NOAH

I put the flowers in the vase and then looked around to survey my work.

Pretty blanket courtesy of Helen, check. Champagne on ice, check. Picnic basket full of delicacies, check.

Satisfied that it looked as good as *I* was going to be able to make it, I took a fortifying breath and left the setup safely in the garden on the side of Helen's shop to go inside and find Summer.

I hadn't yet been introduced to Helen when I dropped in to ask her if I could use the space to surprise Summer. She'd been thrilled to help, and I could tell she was as fond of Summer as Summer was of her.

The door jingled as I walked inside and I looked around the pretty, frilly space to find the woman who was driving me to distraction. It had been a few weeks since the dinner when I'd realized my feelings and we'd spent every possible free moment together since. The more time went on, the more my feelings solidified, and I was finally ready to declare my love to her.

I just hoped she didn't think it was too soon.

This was the kind of thing that would either propel our relationship to new heights or leave me dejected and alone.

Shake it off, Noah, I thought, not wanting to psyche myself out before I did what I'd come to do.

"Noah?" I'd been so stuck in my head I hadn't seen Summer until she was right upon me.

"Hey," I said, my nerves leaving me at the sight of her happy smile.

"What are you doing here?"

"I came by to take you to lunch," I replied, taking her hand in mine. "I hope that's okay."

"It's more than okay, it's perfect," she said, leaning in and tilting her head back for a kiss.

I love it when she does that.

"Great, I'll just wander around until you're ready."

She nodded and spun around, and I browsed the store while I waited.

A few minutes later, Summer came bouncing over to me and said, "I'm ready."

We went outside, and when I led her around the building to the garden, nerves hit me once more.

"Oh my gosh, what's all this?" Summer cried when she saw the picnic setup.

"I know you don't get a lot of time for your break, so I thought it would be easier if I brought the meal to you," I said, taking her hand and helping her onto the blanket.

"This is gorgeous. You really outdid yourself, Mr. Mason," Summer said as I sat next to her.

"I aim to please," I said, handing her a glass and then pouring the champagne I'd already opened.

"Champagne, wow. Are we celebrating something?" she asked, before taking a sip.

I poured some into my own glass and then looked into her green eyes intently.

"Summer," I began, pausing to clear my throat. "I know we've only known each other a few months, but even in that short period, I've come to cherish our time together."

"Me, too," she said, softly.

"I've never felt about anyone the way I feel about you," I admitted, struggling to keep the emotion out of my voice and get out all I'd practiced saying. "I find myself daydreaming in class about your smile, your laugh, and the way you make every space sparkle. As I fall asleep, I replay our conversations in my mind and inevitably dream about you. You're the kindest, sweetest person I've ever met, and I can't believe we're sitting here because *you* wanted to pursue *me*. It defies the laws of nature,"

I paused to take her hand in mine and bring it to my lips.

"What I'm trying to say, is that I'm falling in love with you. Trent told me that when I knew I should shout it from the rooftops, but the only person I need to say it to, is you. You're a gift I know I don't deserve, but I desperately want to keep."

"Noah," Summer whispered, her breath catching as she cried softly. "You say the most beautiful things."

"I don't want you to feel like you have to reciprocate my feelings, I know it's early yet. But I wanted you to know where I'm at, and for you to know I take this relationship seriously. I'm enjoying getting to know you every second and there's no one else I want to be with."

She put her glass down on the ground behind her and launched herself into my arms.

I laughed as she rained kisses all over my face.

"Are you kidding?" she asked between kisses. "I have been falling for you since the second I saw the picture of you on my phone, in that tweed jacket and those sexy glasses. I knew we'd be great together."

"You think my glasses are sexy?" I asked.

Summer looked down at me and nodded. "Oh, yeah, completely."

"Good to know," I said, tucking this new information away for use at a later date.

"You are so sweet. Planning this whole thing for me? I've never had anyone do something so romantic."

"You deserve all the romance the universe has to offer."

She dipped her head then and sealed our declarations with a long, slow, enticing kiss.

"Mmmm. I'm suddenly starving," she said, breaking our embrace and moving to open the basket.

I was now starving as well, but not for food.

Unfortunately, it wasn't the time or the place, so I got my libido in check and helped Summer make our plates.

Fresh fruit, cheese, and paninis from a local eatery were consumed with a gusto. Who knew proclamations could make a person so famished? Once we'd eaten everything in sight, we packed up and stood so Summer could go back to work.

"Thank you for this," Summer said, throwing her arms around my waist and hugging me tight.

"You're welcome," I replied, looking down into her upturned face. "I love you, Summer."

"And I love you, Noah," she said sunnily.

And just like that, it was the best day of my life.

25

SUMMER

Margo and I had gone all out planning Whitney's bachelorette party.

We'd started the day with a pole dancing class. Which was as hilarious as it was informative. Once I got over feeling self-conscious, I'd learned some moves that I was excited to try out on Noah later.

After the class we'd showered and gotten ready for the rest of the evening, which involved vineyard hopping and a lovely outdoor dinner at one of the venues. Our group was small, but we were having a fantastic time.

It included me, Whit, and Margo, of course, as well as Luca's sister Charlotte, their sister-in-law, Sara, and a couple ladies who worked with Whitney.

The champagne was once again flowing as we rode in the limo to our first destination.

"Don't be surprised if Luca sends you both gift baskets tomorrow," Whitney said with a light laugh. "He's going to be feeling really generous after I show him what I learned in that pole dancing class."

Sara nodded and said, "Vanni will pitch in."

"I'm so happy you liked it," I said, shooting a satisfied look at Margo. "Margo thought I was nuts when I brought it up."

"I stand corrected," she replied, raising her glass at me.

I mirrored the gesture and nestled back into my seat.

"This limo is so comfy," I said, turning toward Charlotte, who was sitting next to me, frowning at her drink, which prompted me to ask, "Are you okay?"

She blinked slowly and shifted to look at me.

Her eyes were incredibly sad.

"I'm sorry. I don't want to bring a downer and ruin Whitney's party."

"You won't," I assured her. "What's going on?"

"I told my husband, Nigel, that I want a divorce."

"Oh, honey, I'm so sorry."

She gave a half shrug and said, "It turns out all of those business trips he was taking was just an excuse to get away from me and Sky and sleep with other women. He'd been distant ever since I told him I was pregnant ... I should have known when I saw how he was with Sky. He rarely held her and never fed or changed her. I just thought he was having a hard time bonding with her because he was away so much."

I placed my hand over hers and squeezed it gently.

"You don't deserve that. You're an incredible woman and Sky is the most adorable little girl."

"Yeah, he sounds like a total fucker," Margo said, leaning around me to look at Charlotte. "You'll both be better off without him."

"Thanks," she replied softly. "And I know that in my head, but my heart's pretty bruised up right now."

"Oh my God," I cried, making Charlotte jump in her seat. "*Sorry*, but I just realized something wonderful."

"What's that?" she asked, her tone skeptical.

"You can be one of us! A member of the *Jilted Wives Club*," I said in a rush of excitement. "We go out to dinner on Thursdays and generally hang out and support each other. You'll be a great fit."

"Totally," Margo agreed, then after a pause asked, "So what does that mean for Whitney? She's not going to be a jilted wife anymore once she's happily married to Luca."

I shook my head and said, "Doesn't matter. Once a member, always a member." Then I clapped my hands and told Charlotte, "This is going to be so great."

"I don't know ... I've got Sky."

"Don't worry, you don't have to come every Thursday, but I promise you'll want to. We have the best time and it's just great to get together and hang out with women who want nothing more than to lift you up, ya know?"

"And I bet your mom would love to watch Sky so you could come," Margo added.

"*Yes*," I agreed. "Give her some grandma time and you some me time."

The limo parked and the chauffer came around to open our door, so I gave her a smile and said, "Just think about it. No pressure."

"Okay, I will."

We were led back to the tasting room where our table was reserved. It was tastefully decorated with flowers and white accents. It was preset with some fruit, cheese, and nuts, and we'd scheduled tastings of their whites, since that was what they were famous for.

Our next stop would be reds, with our final stop having dinner and the wine selection being each individual's choice.

By the time we reached our final vineyard, we were all feeling pretty good, so Margo and I requested bread and dipping oil for the table so we could try and soak some of the alcohol up.

Margo and I sandwiched Whitney, her soon-to-be sister-in-law sat across from us, and everyone else filled in around the table.

"Thank you both so much for today, it has been so much

fun," Whitney said, her cheeks rosy from all the wine and champagne.

"We were happy to. Thanks so much for asking us," I told her.

"Yeah, it was a blast. And you deserve it, Whit. You deserve the best of everything," Margo added.

Whitney's eyes got misty. "You two are the best friends a girl could ever have."

"Oh," I cried, getting emotional myself.

"Don't you dare. Either of you. No sap," Margo ordered.

"Okay, but before the no-sap rule goes into effect, can I tell you that Noah and I said *I love you* to each other for the first time? He planned this whole picnic out to tell me. It was the sweetest thing ever."

"That makes me so happy," Whitney said, now weeping slightly.

"Jeez, go ahead," Margo said. "But only a few tears and then you're both cut off, got it?"

Whitney and I nodded.

"It's nice to know the professor's got game," Margo said, raising a glass as Whit and I gave each other a quick hug.

26

NOAH

I was sitting in my chair drinking scotch neat and reading when I heard a knock on my door.

After checking the time, I got up and went to see who could be on my porch at such a late hour.

When I looked out, I saw Summer, bouncing from foot to foot as she waited.

"Hey," I called when I opened the door. The last I'd heard from her, the bachelorette party was in full swing.

I heard a few cat calls and looked out to the street to see about a half-dozen women hanging out of a limo.

"Yeah, Summer ... get some."

"Aww, he's a cutie."

"Get it, girl!"

Those were just a few of the phrases I made out before I was propelled backward as Summer crashed into me and shut the door behind us.

"Hi," Summer mumbled against my neck, before adding, "I really have to pee."

Suddenly, I was standing alone in my entryway, while Summer ran like a flash to the nearest bathroom.

I chuckled and headed back to my chair to wait for Summer to return.

"Sorry about that," she said as she came into the room. Her cheeks were rosy and eyes a little glassy as she looked me over. "Aren't you the cutest thing. Is that a robe?"

I looked down at the robe, which was covering my pajamas, and said, "Yes."

"Oh my gosh, and the glasses too? You're killing me here."

"I am?" I asked, unsure how a robe and glasses were getting this sort of reaction.

"Mmm-hmm," she replied, nodding almost too enthusiastically. "I learned some stuff today."

"About wine?" I asked, since I knew they'd gone to a few tastings.

Summer shook her head and took her phone out of her purse before flinging the purse onto the nearest surface. Seconds later, music strained out of the phone speaker, and she put it down.

Then she began to move.

It only took one swipe of her hands down her body for me to realize where this was going. I knew I could be slow on the uptake sometimes, but I didn't know a man alive who wouldn't understand what was happening.

"Did you also go to a strip club," I croaked.

Summer started unwrapping her dress in the most interesting fashion. *Huh, who knew a dress could do that?* She even spun around slowly, teasing me with bits of exposed flesh, until the material floated away, and she stood before me in the most amazing corset and garter set in an angelic white.

"No. Pole dancing class."

Her hips were moving, and so were her hands ... over those beautiful breasts and back down again.

"I'm afraid I don't have a pole," I managed to say, truly regretting it.

"Guess I'll just have to improvise," she said, stepping toward me and adding, "Stand up."

I did so, quickly and eagerly.

Summer reached for the tie around my waist, never stopping her movement to the music, undoing it, and reaching up to push the robe off of my shoulders. I was left in a plain white T-shirt and plaid pajama pants ... certainly not even close to the level of sexy as what she was wearing. But she didn't seem to mind.

She danced around me with surprisingly great rhythm. I mean, I'd seen her dance at the country bar, but I'd never seen her do anything like this.

It was quite erotic.

I itched to touch, her getup driving me mad, but I didn't want to interrupt the show she was so intent on giving. I was pretty sure it was turning her on as much as it was me, so I was game to be her pole for as long as she wanted.

When she crouched down and then slowly slithered her way up, lightly grazing my body as she did, I hardened to steel-level proportions and had to briefly close my eyes and recite the periodic table in order in my head.

"Noah," Summer whispered, and I felt her hand brushing over the length of me.

My eyes flew open.

"Shall we go to your room?"

Rather than answer, I picked her up and practically sprinted down the hall toward my bedroom.

Her gales of laughter followed us through the house, and by the time I deposited her on my bed, my body was on fire.

She moved back onto the bed and propped herself up on her elbows while I quickly rid myself of my clothes. This time I stood before her fully naked, while her hungry gaze traveled over my body.

When she moved to unzip the side of her corset, I begged, "No, *please*, keep it on."

Her hands fell back, and I reached for the strings on either side of her hips, then ripped the fabric and gathered the material to throw her panties to the side.

"I'll buy more," I promised, moving over her and dipping my head to finally give her a kiss.

When we broke apart, we were both left gasping for breath, and Summer said, "You liked my dance."

I positioned myself between her legs, grasped her hips with my hands, and slid swiftly and deeply inside of her. When I was fully seated, I looked into her lust-filled eyes and said, "I loved it." I bent to kiss her again and whispered, "I love *you*," against her lips. And then I began to move.

27
SUMMER

I woke up feeling satisfied and surprisingly *not* hung over.

Noah was sleeping soundly and looked so delightfully sweet and rumpled I just had to give him a blow job.

It was Sunday, after all, and neither of us had anything to do but laze around and enjoy each other all day, so I figured I'd start us off right.

Noah woke making the most delicious sounds, and when I was done, he gave me a whopper of a kiss and then promptly passed back out. I decided to let him sleep and go make us a decadent Sunday breakfast.

I scurried through the house, cognizant of the fact the air was cooling my naked bottom, eager to find my dress. Once I was clothed, save for my still-bare bottom, I went to the kitchen in search of a pan.

I put on Spotify and then started getting out all of the ingredients to make French toast with blueberries, cheesy scrambled eggs, and bacon.

I sang along with Sia as I prepared everything, feeling pretty fantastic about the current state of my life. Helen was interested in making some of my designs and giving them a shot in her store. Whitney's wedding was just around the corner. We may have a new member to the already fabulous *Jilted Wives Club*. And I was in love with a man who made a bathrobe look sexy.

It's a great time to be me!

Once it was done, I plated everything up on his white square plates and took them into the bedroom.

"Hey, sleepyhead," I called as I entered the room.

Noah shifted and turned his head toward the sound of my voice, then opened one eye.

When he saw the plates steaming with food, he sniffed at the air and sat up. "Breakfast?"

"I hope you're hungry," I said as I laid his plate on his lap.

"*Hmm*, famished," he mumbled tiredly, before looking at me and saying, "Aww, you're dressed."

"Well, I couldn't very well cook without underwear," I teased, taking the syrup from under my arm and handing it to him.

Noah flushed and said, "Oh ... right. Sorry about that."

"Believe me, I have no complaints," I said with a chuckle as I joined him on the bed.

"I can't believe I had the stuff to make all this."

"Your pantry and fridge are both pretty well-stocked."

"Huh, well, thanks for making breakfast," Noah said, then put a forkful of French toast in his mouth. "Mmmm."

"I hope you don't mind me crashing your weekend," I said, looking at him from under my lashes to gauge his reaction.

"No, not at all," he replied, completely focused on his food. "I didn't have anything going on and it was quite a treat to have you show up on my porch last night. It looked like everyone was having a good time."

I laughed as I remembered the ladies shouting affirmations from the limo.

"We really did. And Whitney seemed to have a blast, which is the most important thing. She wasn't so sure she wanted all the trimmings and parties since this is her second wedding, but we've all done our best to make sure we celebrated her and Luca, while adhering to her wishes."

"I look forward to meeting them," he said, glancing over at me as he asked, "Is she like Margo?"

I shook my head and smiled. "No, not at all. Margo is one of a kind."

"She's a bit intimidating," he whispered, as if she may somehow overhear.

"She's a pussycat. I swear."

He raised his eyebrows and gave me a look of disbelief, which made me laugh.

"Okay, maybe a baby lion," I amended. "But, no, Whitney is more laid back. She's raised two kids and works in accounting. She's just the sweetest and her and Luca together are perfect. You're going to love them, promise."

"I find it interesting how different you all seem to be. Yet, you're very close."

"Yeah, we are, but for some reason ... it works. It was the luckiest day of my life when I decided to go to that support group meeting, which I hated, and ended up meeting the two of them. Margo literally ran me over, she was trying to get out of there so fast," I said, laughing at the memory.

"And you formed a sort-of club..."

"The *Jilted Wives Club*. I came up with the name because it was the one thing we had in common. Sort of tied us together initially, but now we're best friends." I hoped he didn't think it sounded lame or childish.

"Clubs are a good way to form bonds and build lasting relationships," Noah said, and my worry eased. "My dad's been in a book club with the same guys for over three decades. And Trent and I were part of a swim club for years."

"Oh, do you still swim?"

"Just for pleasure really now. And exercise. Once we both began to work full time and really strive for promotions, and then Cam got pregnant, we realized we needed to free up some time in our schedule, so the swim club was the thing we could let go."

I nodded but chewed on my lip as I worried with our lives changing, that maybe the ladies wouldn't have time for our club anymore.

"I'm sure that won't be the case with you," Noah said, picking up on my distress. "You are all friends and that won't change, no matter who gets married, or how your lives evolve. Trent and I still hang out all the time, we simply don't swim with the club anymore."

"That makes sense," I said, pleased he was so intuitive. "So, what do you think we should do today? Stay in and watch TV, go for a hike, maybe check out a farmer's market?"

Noah put his empty plate on the end table and turned to reach for me.

"I think we should spend the day in bed."

I have to agree, that sounds perfect.

28

NOAH

"Hey, I'm Luca, it's nice to meet you."

"Noah," I replied, shaking the friendly looking gentleman's hand.

He was just a touch shorter than me, with dark hair and eyes and an easy grin. He draped his arm over Whitney's shoulders, and had a glass of red wine in his free hand.

"This is a special treat," Luca said, giving his intended a loving glance. "The ladies are very protective of their Thursday night dinners."

"I'm pretty sure they wanted the chance to give me the third degree in person," I joked. "Make sure I'm good enough for Summer."

"He figured you out, babe," Luca told Whitney with a grin.

She slapped his chest and said, "Stop." Then she looked at me and said, "I did ask Summer to invite you because I wanted to meet you before the wedding. I know we'll be so busy, and I thought a preemptive meet was in order. And I thought you'd feel more comfortable with Luca along."

"Yeah, when I met them, I was the only man present. It was quite intimidating."

"Please," Margo said, rolling her eyes. "You *love* being the only man in a room full of women."

Luca shrugged and said, "It's true."

I chuckled and pulled out a chair for Summer when she approached the table.

"Sorry, I had to use the little girl's room," she said, moving to give everyone a quick hug and kiss before she sat at gave me a happy look. "Thanks."

I took the seat next to her, which was across from the happy couple and next to Margo.

"It's so good to see you, Luca," Summer said, leaning across the table toward him. "I bet you're so busy with the business and the wedding. Can you believe it's already next weekend? The Castle is so gorgeous, I know your wedding is going to be *the* event of the year. I'm so excited."

"I think she's more excited about the wedding than you two are," Margo joked, and I couldn't help but chuckle.

Whenever the subject of the upcoming nuptials came up, Summer oohed and aahed and practically floated around the room.

Luca laughed heartily.

"It's great seeing you, too, Summer. It's hard to believe the wedding is just around the corner, but I have been lucky to have Whit and my family pretty much taking care of everything. All I really have to do is show up on time and the rest will be done."

"It's all his mom, I haven't done much either," Whitney said, laying her head against Luca's shoulder.

They looked great together and really had the glow of love surrounding them.

"Sounds perfect. If I ever get married again, I'm hiring your mom," Margo said as she tossed back her drink and signaled the waiter to bring another.

"Not me," Summer said, her voice getting that dreamy quality. "I have a vision board for my wedding and all kinds of ideas."

"You didn't have a big to-do with Jared?" Whitney asked,

then shot me a pained look as if she were sorry she'd brought up Summer's ex.

I gave a slight wave of my hand to indicate I wasn't worried about it, and her face cleared.

"No, he'd had a big wedding with his first wife, and didn't want to go through it again, so we were married in Vegas."

"What about you, Noah?" Margo asked, taking the focus off Summer and bringing me into the conversation. "Have you always dreamed of a big wedding, or do you plan to have the hands-off approach like Luca?"

"Honestly, no one has ever asked me that before," I replied sheepishly. "I guess, thinking about it now, I'd like to have some input, but would defer most of the decisions to my bride-to-be, since she's obviously been dreaming about it for a long time."

Margo's lips turned up and I realized my answer indicated Summer would be the bride in my scenario.

I cleared my throat and amended, "At least, that's my assumption."

Margo gave a joyful chuckle and shot me a wink.

Maybe she isn't so scary after all.

"So, Summer tells me the two of you are in accounting?" I asked, hoping to successfully change the subject.

"That's right," Luca replied. "My father started the firm where Whit and I work. It's becoming a true family affair since Stella has started working with us after school. She's got a real brain for numbers, just like her mom."

"Good for her. It's never too early to get your foot in the door," Margo said.

"And you're an English professor. How do you like that?" Whitney asked.

"I love it, most of the time."

"When don't you love it?" Luca asked.

"Toward the end of the year. Finals ... and everyone scrambling to make up the work they'd procrastinated doing all semester long," I replied with a rueful grin.

"I bet you were one of those students who did their homework right away and never procrastinated," Summer said, tipping her head back to look up at me.

She had that look on her face. The one she got when she wanted a kiss. So, I complied, leaning over to brush my lips against hers. I'd intended for it to be an innocent peck, but upon contact Summer's lips parted and I couldn't ignore the invitation.

I realized we were getting overheated when a low whistle sounded at the table.

We broke apart to see everyone watching us unabashedly.

"That's what I'm talking about," Luca said, then glanced at Margo and asked, "When are we going to make this a sixsome?"

"When hell freezes over," Margo retorted. "Is that even a word? It sounds borderline sexual."

"Yes, it's a word. It's like a foursome, but with six people."

"If you say so..."

29
SUMMER

"This is more beautiful than I'd imagined, and my imagination is pretty extensive."

I looked around The Castle, my head swiveling as I took in every ornate detail inside and outside.

The wedding itself had been an intimate affair, with only friends and family in attendance at the church. Sure, Luca's family was pretty huge on its own, but the rest of the guests were invited to join the newlyweds at The Castle for the reception.

Whitney had looked absolutely splendid, and the expression on Luca's face as she walked down the aisle toward him had made my vow to not cry impossible. Luckily, before I'd left him for my own procession down the aisle, Noah had tucked a handkerchief into my palm, and I'd stashed it in my bouquet.

I hadn't been the only one in tears at the church. Whitney, Luca, Luca's mom, Stella, and Charlotte had all indulged in some sniffles. I swear I even saw Margo tear up, although she denied it.

Now Noah and I were exploring The Castle, hand in hand, as he indulged me.

"It's quite spectacular," he said as we moved through the rooms.

"Wait until you see the grounds where her reception is being held. I took a sneak peek when we were all getting ready. It's glorious." It was an absolute fairy tale wedding. Similar to what I would want if I ever got married again. Of course, I wouldn't copy Whitney, but I had some ideas. And Noah's comment about wanting input into his wedding, even though he'd mostly defer to his bride, while he'd been looking at me with his sweet doe eyes, had definitely gotten me daydreaming about the wedding of my dreams.

"I have to say, this color is quite lovely on you. I can't quite pinpoint the shade of blue, but I've been admiring it on you all afternoon."

"Aww, thanks, honey," I said, pausing to gauge his reaction at the endearment. I'd never been one for sweet nicknames like that, probably because I'd called Jared, *babe*, once and he'd told me to never call him by anything other than his given name. When Noah didn't flinch, or show any signs of disgust, I figured he was okay with it. "It's called dusty blue. You'll see we totally match the theme once we get outside."

"It's beautiful."

"Thank you. It has pockets!" I exclaimed, causing Noah to laugh.

I really was in love with the dress. It was described as crepe-back satin with one-shoulder. It was floor length with a generous slit over the left leg, and it made me feel like a princess.

"Why do women always seem to get excited about a dress with pockets? Even my mother mentioned it to me about the gown she wore to my promotion," Noah asked, sounding truly baffled.

"It's one of those simple pleasures. Somewhere to put our hands, or a tube of lipstick ... I don't know, it just makes me happy."

"Good enough," Noah said, leaning down to drop a kiss on my forehead.

He'd been doing cute things like that all day. Paranoid about messing up my hair or makeup, but still wanting to be affectionate.

"There you are," Margo said as she glided toward us. Her dress was similar to mine but was an A-line V-neck that showcased her breasts beautifully. "They want to get started."

"Okay," I said, lacing my fingers through Noah's as we joined Margo and started outside.

Whitney had decided to forgo any kind of head table, instead choosing to go with various large round tables. The tables had white table clothes with dusty-blue linens and gold accent pieces. The centerpieces were fern and eucalyptus. Elegant and classy through and through.

Noah and I joined Margo at table two as the festivities began.

Cheers erupted as Luca and Whitney walked out of the castle and onto the dance floor. *Return to Love* by Andrea Bocelli featuring Ellie Goulding began to play through the speakers, and Luca swept Whitney into his arms, and they began to glide across the floor.

"*What*?" I breathed, holding a hand to my chest as I stood up so I could see better. "Did they take lessons?"

I glanced over at Margo, who was grinning back at me, then looked back at the dance floor.

"They're magnificent."

When the song ended, Luca dipped Whitney, before bringing her back up to kiss her soundly. She threw her arms around his neck, and everyone started to clap.

"*Oh my gosh*," I cried, looking at Noah, who was looking warmly down at me.

"You didn't know?" he asked.

I shook my head and wiped under my eyes, hoping my mascara hadn't run.

The excitement died down as everyone took their seats and dinner service began. Steak, fish, fingerling potatoes, and steamed vegetables were occasionally interrupted by the clinking of glasses, which Whit and Luca indulged with lots of kisses.

Once the dancing began, Noah turned to me and asked, "May I have this dance?"

"Absolutely," I replied, placing my hand in his and letting him lead me onto the floor.

"Not quite a two-stepping song," he said wryly as we began to move to the music.

"No, but this is nice, being in your arms," I replied, looking up at him as I moved in even closer.

"Yeah," he agreed, then pulled me in so I could rest my cheek against his chest and hug him tightly.

"This is wonderful," I said with a sigh.

I loved how safe and secure I felt being in his arms.

"It is," he murmured, the words rumbling against my cheek.

"Okay, move over. I'm cutting in," I heard Margo say from behind me and realized the song had stopped and was transitioning into a new one.

"Me or him?" I asked her.

"I'm talking to Noah, you're the one I wanna dance with," she said, already starting to move to the more upbeat tune.

"Uh, yeah, I'll leave you guys to it," Noah said, leaving the dance floor as fast as his legs could take him.

I watched him with a smile.

"He's more of a country line dancer," I told Margo.

"I know," she said, taking my hands. "Now, shake that ass."

30

NOAH

I took the tote bag with fresh chicken noodle soup, Sprite, crackers, and gummy bears out of my car, before locking it and making my way to Summer's apartment.

It was a few weeks since the wedding and she'd come down with the flu a few days ago. I'd come by to check on her when I could, but since it was the end of the semester and my busiest time of year, I'd been staying at my place at night.

I felt terrible every time I left her because she looked so sick and sad. Totally un-Summer-like.

My mom had stopped by yesterday while I was at work to check on her, which really warmed my heart and kind of solidified the fact in my mind that Summer would make a great addition to our family.

It was something I'd been thinking about a lot lately, but with Summer getting sick, I hadn't had a chance to do anything other than ponder it myself.

At her door, I shuffled everything into one hand so I could unlock the door with the spare key Summer had given me. We'd swapped keys a few days ago, and it was my first time using hers. But, as I started to push it open, I met resistance and it was slammed back in my face.

"What the heck?" I muttered, stumbling back before calling out, "Summer?"

"What do you want?" a harsh voice, one that was definitely *not* Summer, asked through the door.

"I'm here to see Summer. I brought her some items to help her feel better," I said, feeling awkward shouting through metal.

The door opened a little and I looked down to see a weathered face staring back at me.

"Hello, uh, ma'am. I'm Noah, Summer's boyfriend." Boyfriend suddenly seemed like such a childish word, and not nearly meaningful enough. "I'm here to see her and give her some soup." When she neither spoke or opened the door farther, I held up my hand and said, "I have a key."

I heard a huff before the door opened slightly and she walked away.

I went in, looking around the space for Summer, but only saw the lady with the scowl.

"Is Summer in her room?" I asked, pointing toward the closed door.

"She's sleeping and you'll not wake her."

O-kay.

I crossed to put the tote bag on the kitchen counter and said, "Like I said earlier, I'm Noah. And you are...?"

"I'm Adelaide, her mother," she said, and then to my horror, lit a cigarette.

"Ma'am, I don't think Summer would appreciate you smoking in here, especially since she's feeling poorly."

Adelaide snorted and muttered, "Well, look at the big balls on this one. *Feeling poorly*? My girl's sick with the flu. And a sick girl wants her mother, not some bumbling giant in a jacket with patches on the sleeves. What's this, the fifties?"

I blinked, confused over the fact that *this* woman had given birth to and raised Summer. It went against the laws of nature.

"You've dropped off your soup, so you can head on out now," she said, when we simply stood there looking at one another.

"I'd really like to look in on Summer..."

"Look here," she said with a scoff. "What my girl doesn't need is another no-account man swooping in with talk of *making her happy* and *giving her the world* and then letting her down. You wouldn't know it by looking at your outfit, but this *ain't* the fifties anymore. Women don't need some man to make them happy. In fact, all men ever seem to do is make us miserable. So, why don't you and your no-good penis git."

My no-good penis?

"Ma'am ... *Adelaide*," I began, hoping I could at least convince this dragon at the gate to let me pass long enough just to make sure Summer was okay in her room. Because with this woman on nursing duty, there was honestly no telling.

"Don't you Adelaide me. I told you, Summer doesn't want to see you and you need to go."

"Summer never said..."

"Well, I'm sayin' it. Get out before I call the cops."

Is this woman for real?

From the expression on her face and the way she was tapping her foot, I was guessing she was. It occurred to me to simply run past her and push my way through the door, but that seemed like an odd and juvenile thing to do.

I'd simply leave and then call Summer to check on her. Then, once her mother was long gone, I'd come back and make sure she ate her soup.

"Okay, there's no need to do anything hasty. I'll go. Just tell Summer I was here."

When she didn't reply, I turned to leave, glancing one last time at the still-closed door.

I left without so much as a *goodbye* or *nice to meet you*, which would shame my mother since she'd raised me to be polite. But, since she also raised me to tell the truth, I figured she might understand.

Once I was back outside, I called Summer, hoping she'd

answer and send her mother packing, but it went straight to voicemail.

As I jogged down the steps, I typed out a text, letting her know I'd been by, her soup was on the counter, and asking her to call when she was able.

When I was about to go to sleep and she still hadn't called, I tried again, but had no luck.

It was the first time in weeks we hadn't told each other *I love you* before going to bed.

31

SUMMER

"I don't know what I'm going to do," I managed in between sobs.

Whitney and Margo were sitting on either side of me on my sofa. We were all in variations of sweats and T-shirts, and they had been listening to me cry for the last thirty minutes.

"Honey, why don't you start at the beginning and tell us exactly what has been going on," Whitney said, rubbing her palm over my back in a circular motion.

I worked on calming myself down so I could speak and actually be coherent this time.

"Late last week I began to feel sick. Nauseous at first, with a headache and some dizziness, and then I began throwing up. I couldn't keep anything down for days ...Noah was really sweet. Calling and checking on me and bringing me stuff, but I just felt so miserable, and nothing helped."

"Okay, and then you said your mom came?" Margo prompted.

"Yeah, the harbinger of death herself," I muttered, then immediately felt guilty. "No, that's not fair. She came by to help me, although I certainly didn't ask her to, but as usual, she made things worse. Not only by making a mess in my apartment and smoking inside, but she was here when Noah came over. I was asleep and didn't even know."

"Oh, Lord. How did that go?" Whit asked.

"According to her he came barging in and throwing his weight around, *just like a man*, and she ended up kicking him out."

"That doesn't sound like Noah."

"Not at all," Margo agreed. "What did Noah say?"

I gave her a sheepish look and said, "I don't know, I haven't actually talked to him since then."

"What? Why not?" Whitney asked.

"Because I'm so embarrassed. I know how horrible my mother can be, why do you think I hadn't introduced him to her yet. I was kinda hoping they'd never have to meet. He met Helen ... that's close enough."

"Honey," Whitney said, her voice full of censure. "Hasn't he tried to get a hold of you?"

I nodded, wringing my hands together, and admitted, "Yes. He's called and even texted a few times, even though he hates it."

"And you've ignored him?"

"It's only been two days," I argued, even though I knew it was wrong. "I texted back and said I was feeling better, and I'd let him know when I was able to talk, but that's it."

"What else is going on, Summer?" Margo asked, giving me a look that said I'd better fess up or else.

I was also *late*.

I fell back against the couch and cried, "*I think I'm pregnant*."

"And that's why you're hiding from Noah," Margo surmised.

"Sweetheart, that's wonderful. I know how much you want to have children," Whitney said sweetly. "I know it's not exactly the way you wanted it to happen, but I'm sure Noah will be thrilled as well. Don't you think so?"

"I don't know. Especially not right after meeting my mother.

I mean, those genes will be in our child, he may not be so keen on that."

"Stop it," Margo said sharply. "It's one thing to be scared to tell him, especially since you haven't been feeling yourself and are hyper-emotional. But you do him, and yourself, a disservice, by talking that kind of nonsense."

At her words, I started crying again. Mostly because I knew she was right, and partly because I hated that she was disappointed in me.

"Hey," she said, making me blink up at her. "You owe me, remember? Big time."

"For what?" Whitney asked.

"That speed dating thing. I said I'd take her place, but she'd owe me one. So, I'm calling in my favor. You're going to stop crying, take a shower, and doll yourself up so you feel better. Then you're going to go to Noah's and talk to him. About your mom and about the possibility you may be pregnant. You'll take a few tests with you, and you can find out together. It's not something you should go through alone and Noah deserves to be a part of it if he wants to."

"Oh, I forgot about that. How'd it go?" I asked.

Margo glared at me, and I shrank back against the couch.

"We can talk about that later. For now, you need to go get yourself cleaned up and call Noah."

"I'm still feeling poorly," I said, hoping to tap into her compassion.

"Eat a cracker," was her reply.

Alrighty then.

I walked slowly to my room, like a dog with her tail tucked between her legs, and turned on the shower.

Once I was done and dressed, I could admit to myself that I felt better, but I wasn't going to say so to Margo.

I walked out of my room to see them putting the last few things away and said, "Oh, you guys didn't have to clean up."

"Don't worry about it, that's what friends are for," Margo said, getting herself right back into my good graces.

"Yeah, sweetie, you've had a rough week and we wanted to help you out at least a little," Whit agreed.

"You guys really are the best," I said, getting a little weepy again.

Dang. I'd always been a girl who cried easily, but this was getting ridiculous.

"Did you talk to Noah?" Margo asked.

"Yeah, just to see if I could come over to talk. He said, *yes*, of course, but he sounded a little guarded." And I'd hated to hear it, especially knowing I'd made him feel that way.

"He'll understand," Whitney assured me. "And you better make sure you call us as soon as you know either way about being pregnant."

"I promise."

32

NOAH

I was nervous.

After the run-in with Summer's mother and then her pretty much going radio silent on me for days, I was feeling unsure of where I stood in this relationship.

Which was concerning, considering the direction *my* thoughts had been heading in terms of *us*.

I grabbed a bongo off one of my shelves and sat down to start beating on it, which was something I often did when I was nervous or needed to clear my head. I had no idea the proper way to play it, but it helped for some reason.

It had just started working when I heard Summer's key in the door, and a few seconds later, the sound of it shutting behind her. Suddenly, the nerves were back full force.

But when she walked into the living room, pale and looking extremely distraught, I forgot about myself and moved quickly to her.

"Hey, are you okay?" I asked, placing my hands on her shoulders and surveying her face.

She looked exhausted and seconds away from weeping.

"I've been better," she replied, attempting levity, and failing. "Can we sit?"

"Yes, of course," I said, ushering her toward the couch. "Can I get you anything? Water ... Sprite?"

"Some water would be good."

Once I'd grabbed her water, I sat beside her on the sofa and waited for her to speak her mind.

"So, I heard you met my mother," Summer began, her eyes wary.

"I did." I didn't want to be rude or disparage her mother, but I wouldn't lie to her either. "I have to say, she wasn't a big fan."

Summer snorted and said, "I'm sure that's an understatement. I'm so sorry you had to meet her that way ... before I got a chance to prepare you and give you insight as to who you'd be dealing with. I told you a little about her already, but I'm sure you still weren't expecting to be met with what I'm sure was great animosity."

"I'm sure she was simply trying to take care of you and protect you," I said, giving her the benefit of the doubt. She was Summer's mother, after all, so she couldn't be all bad.

"That's sweet, but when it comes to my mother, her thoughts and actions are usually selfish. It took me a long time to come to terms with that, but, unfortunately, it's the truth."

"I'm sorry," I said, unsure what else I *could* say. "But besides that, how have you been? You haven't said much the last few days ... I wanted to come by and check on you."

"I know ... and I hate that I kept you waiting and probably made you feel confused. I mean, she was terrible to me, and I was the one she was supposed to be taking care of; I can only imagine the things she said to you. I wish I'd been awake and knew you were there, so we could have avoided most of it."

"It's fine. I'm not in love with your mother," I assured her, watching her intently for any indication her feelings had changed.

Summer swallowed and seemed to get paler.

"Do you have any crackers? I'm still a bit nauseous."

"Oh, uh, let me go check. I'm sure I have something."

I hurried into the kitchen and checked the pantry, shouting out, "Got some," before grabbing the box and taking them to her.

"Here you go," I said, handing her a sleeve of Saltines. "Have you been to the doctor?"

She shook her head slightly and said, "I couldn't get an appointment until tomorrow."

"What time? Would you like me to take you?" I offered, wanting to help her in any way I could.

I hoped I could convince her to stay with me tonight, so I could take care of her. I'd hated being away from her the last few days, knowing she was feeling poorly and hopeless to do anything about it.

"Actually, that would be great. The appointment is at eight in the morning," she said, her lips curving up for the first time since she'd entered the house.

Relief flooded me.

"Noah, there's something else I need to discuss with you," she said, her eyes intent on mine. "I don't want you to freak out, because I don't even know anything for sure yet, but my gut is literally telling me it's a strong possibility."

"What is it?" I asked, taking her hand in mine to try and ease some of her distress.

"Well, in addition to the nausea, vomiting, headaches, fatigue, and light-headedness ... I'm late."

"For?"

Summer looked at me nervously and said, "My period."

I'm embarrassed to say it took a few beats for me to connect the dots, and when I did, all I said was, "*Oh*!"

Wow, she thinks she could be pregnant? I momentarily lost the ability to breathe at the possibility.

"Yeah, *oh*," she said, with a light laugh. "Like I said, I don't know anything for sure, but I did bring a few tests with me so that we can find out together, if you want."

My brain was scrambling to catch up, while my stomach was

churning, and my heart started yearning. A million emotions ran through me all at once, but the one that was prevalent? *Hope.*

"A few?" I asked, wondering why we'd need more than one.

"Yeah. Sometimes there's a false negative, or positive. So, I figured if I took three, we could go with the majority. Of course, we will find out *for sure* for sure, at the doctor tomorrow."

"Great, what do we need to do?"

"Well, *I* need to pee on a few sticks. All you have to do is hold my hand while we wait for the results."

"I can do that," I assured her, then took her hand and led her to the bathroom to do just that.

33
SUMMER

I shut the bathroom door and rushed to the toilet to throw up.

Ugh, how embarrassing. It's bad enough Noah is going to be waiting on the other side of the door while I pee on a stick, but now he got to listen to me vomit as well ... There goes the mystery.

If I was pregnant, I knew he'd be witness to a whole lot more, so I tried not to let it bother me too much.

We're all human, right? And bodily functions are a part of life.

Still, as I rinsed my mouth out in the sink and opened the pregnancy tests and laid them all out on the back of the toilet, I wished we'd had a little bit longer together with the mystery.

With a glance at the door, I sat down and did what I had to do, then placed each stick on top of a box and finished up before opening the door to find Noah pacing the hallway.

"You okay?" I asked, noting the panicked look in his eyes.

"Mm-hm, I'm good. You?" he asked, moving to stand right in front of me. "Want me to go get the crackers?"

I flushed at the knowledge that he'd *definitely* heard the puking.

"No, thanks, I'm okay right now."

He nodded profusely, and asked, "So how long do we wait?"

"About three minutes."

"Okay. Okay. Okay." Noah muttered, lifting his arm to presumably set a timer on his watch.

I bit my cheek to keep from laughing. It wasn't a funny situation by any means, but Noah was just so adorable I couldn't help myself.

"How are finals going?" I asked, hoping to distract him.

"Good, only a couple more this week and we will be wrapping up this semester," he said absently, his eyes never leaving his watch.

After a few seconds of silence, I felt the need to fill the space and said, "I saw Margo and Whitney earlier. They're both doing good."

"Oh, yeah? That's nice."

"Noah," I prompted.

"Huh?" he asked, still not looking up, then said, "Three minutes is a really long time."

"When you're watching the clock it is," I joked, putting my hand on his arm. "Hey."

Noah glanced at me with unfocused eyes.

"It's going to be okay ... either way."

His expression cleared and he gave me a small smile as he let out a breath.

"Yeah, it will be." Then his alarm sounded, and he shouted, "*It's time*!" making me jump and press my hand to my heart.

We walked into the bathroom and stood side by side as we both bent slightly to look down at the three tests.

Three plus signs stared back at us.

We both sank down to the floor.

"That's pretty definitive," Noah said softly.

"I'd say so," I agreed. "Of course, tomorrow we will know for sure..."

"But we kind of know for sure right now."

"Yup."

We sat in silence for a few minutes and as I really thought

about it, about the fact I was pregnant and going to have a baby, something I had wanted for years, excitement started to grow inside of me.

"*Oh my gosh*," I said, covering my mouth as I let out a startled laugh. "*I'm going to have a baby*!"

"*Me, too*!" Noah exclaimed, and we turned to look at each other.

"*Holy Toledo*," I said, which made him laugh.

"A family," he said.

I let out an exaggerated breath as my mind began to spin.

"Okay ... *okay*. I have money saved for a place, so I can move before the baby comes. I don't want her to grow up in that apartment. She should have a yard ... oh, we can get a dog!"

"Wait," Noah said, holding up a hand. "I have room here. You should move in with me. I have a yard, and room for a dog. That way we would be together ... to raise her together. It's perfect."

I blinked and stared at him, because seriously ... *this man*.

"You are so sweet, but we probably shouldn't get ahead of ourselves, right?" I asked gently. "We're excited, but we do have time to figure this out. Let's go to the doctor and find out for sure before we worry about what comes next. Okay?"

"Yeah, sure, of course ... just putting it out there," Noah said, running a hand through his hair. "I want you to know it's an option. That I'm in this, one-thousand percent. I love you and I want us to be a real family."

"I love you, too," I said, crawling over to get in his lap.

He bent his head and gave me the sweetest kiss I've ever felt. It was full of love and promise, and pure joy.

Pulling back slightly, he whispered against my lips, "I'm really happy."

"Me, too," I whispered back, then bridged the gap and kissed him again.

A phone started ringing in the other room and I recognized my ringtone.

"It's probably Whit or Margo, they knew we were going to take a test and are probably dying to know the results."

Noah helped me up off the floor and asked, "So, we're telling people? I've got to call my parents."

I paused and asked, "Should we wait? Is it bad to tell people this early?"

"It's never bad to share joy with the people you love," he replied.

I stepped toward him, fisted my hand in his shirt, and urged him down for another kiss.

"I *really* do love you."

34

NOAH

I held my breath as I waited, trying to keep my attention focused on the monitor and ignore the fact the doctor was using a *vaginal* ultrasound to see the baby.

We'd gotten confirmation via blood work that Summer was indeed pregnant and had promptly made an appointment with an OB doctor. Luckily, my sister-in-law, Jamilla, had given us a recommendation for an OB clinic she'd used and loved, and we were able to get right in.

Suddenly, a bubble with a large head inside of it popped on the screen, and my heart stopped.

Then the doctor pressed a button and the room filled with a whooshing sound.

"That's the baby's heartbeat," she said with a smile.

I squeezed Summer's hand in mine, not even bothering to fight back the tears that threatened.

"It's beautiful," Summer said, quietly weeping.

"Amazing," I agreed.

"It looks like you're about six weeks along, so it's early yet, but everything looks great. I'll print out some pictures for you."

"Thank you," I said, unable to tear my eyes from the screen.

"So much," Summer added.

"I'll leave you to get dressed," the doctor said, leaving the monitor on so it was frozen on the picture of the baby.

As Summer got up and put her clothes on, I found myself mesmerized by that fuzzy screen.

"Such a miracle," I mused.

"Isn't it?" Summer said, coming up behind me and wrapping her arms around my waist. "I can't believe I'm growing an actual human being in my body."

"Such a gift."

She rested her cheek briefly against my back and said, "Ready?"

I nodded and we left the room to go make our next appointment before leaving the clinic.

"Do you mind if we stop by my parents' house on the way?" I asked, once we were in the car.

"Of course not," she replied.

My parents were both thrilled at the prospect of being grandparents again and my mother in particular had been dying for me to bring Summer by.

Fifteen minutes later, we were parking in my parents' driveway.

"They are going to love these photos," I said excitedly as I opened the passenger door and helped Summer out.

Before we made it up the walkway to the door, it swung open and my parents both came barreling out.

"There she is," my father said boastfully, moving to take Summer in for a bear hug.

"Hi," Summer managed.

"Don't suffocate the poor girl," my mom said, patting him on the back and then pulling Summer into her arms once she was free. "Oh, Summer, you precious woman."

Summer looked slightly embarrassed, and I hoped also pleased, at my parents' affection and enthusiasm.

"Come inside," my mother said, not completely letting Summer go by tucking her arm through Summer's. "How does some tea sound?"

"Wonderful, thank you," Summer replied.

My father fell into step beside me as we followed them into the house.

"Your mother is beside herself at the prospect of another grandchild," he told me in a hushed tone.

"I know. She's been sending me pictures of baby clothes and links to cribs. She's going off the rails," I said with a laugh.

"Oh, let her have her fun. I hope your girl is ready for hurricane grandma."

"Actually, I think she'll love it. I'm not sure how her mom will react about the news, Summer is putting off telling her, but I think she'll appreciate how happy Mom is about it and how much she'll want to be involved. At least, I hope so."

"If it gets to be too much, just let me know and I'll tell your mom to ease up."

We found them in the kitchen, my mother preparing a tray of tea and scones, and Summer at the table.

"How is the nausea doing, any better?" my mother was asking.

"Much. At least I'm not sick all the time anymore," Summer replied. "Now it's mostly occasional nausea."

"Well, I picked up some ginger tea and these pregnancy pops that you can suck on to help with the nausea."

"That's so sweet of you, thank you," Summer said, her eyes meeting mine. "Noah, why don't you show them the pictures."

"There are pictures?" my mom asked, forgetting all about what she was doing to round the island and come to me.

I pulled out the small, flimsy, grainy shots and held them out. My parents oohed and aahed like they were portraits taken by Annie Leibovitz.

"This child is going to be a beaut," my father proclaimed, making me laugh.

"How can you tell?"

"Look at his or her parents. *Hell*, look at the grandparents," he replied with a grin. "Gonna be a showstopper."

I caught Summer's gaze from over his head and rolled my eyes genially.

"I'm going to babysit all the time," my mother said happily.

"We're going to hold you to it," I replied.

35

SUMMER

"No booze for you, baby mamma," Margo said, skipping my glass as she poured wine.

I pouted and admitted, "I hadn't really thought about that." But now that everyone around me was drinking, I began to realize it was only the first of many things I would be giving up during my pregnancy and beyond.

"Speaking of ... I brought you these books I used while I was pregnant with Sky. I hope you don't mind, Whitney told me," Charlotte said, handing me a tote bag of books.

"I knew Char was coming tonight, and although I know you aren't telling everyone yet, I figured it would come up tonight, *a lot*," Whitney said with a laugh. "And since she's in the club now, I didn't think you'd mind."

"No, of course, it's completely cool," I assured them both, giving Charlotte a welcoming smile. "I'm so excited you decided to join us."

"Honestly, I've been going kind of crazy being either at work or home, with no breaks or anything, even though with Nigel gone all the time, things are pretty much the same. So, when Whit told me you were all going out tonight, I called my mom and asked her to watch Sky ... and here we are. I do appreciate you guys including me."

"Anytime, and I gotta say, your hair looks fab," Margo said, lifting her glass in appreciation.

"Oh, thanks," Charlotte said, her hand going up to touch the end of her straight bob. "I needed something quick and easy. With Sky and work, I don't have time for a lot of prep, and I can't go to the gallery every day with my hair in a bun, so ... this was what my stylist came up with."

"It really suits you," Whitney told her new sister-in-law.

"Ladies, have you had a chance to look over the menu?" our server asked, putting a pause on the conversation.

I'd had a craving for beef, so we were at a new farm-to-table steakhouse, which I was really excited about. It was kind of crazy, because it seemed like I was either stuffing my face, or too nauseous to eat anything. There was no in between.

Luckily tonight, I was starving.

"You seem to be feeling better," Whitney said once we were alone again.

"Much, *thank God*. I don't know if I would have been able to handle nine months of that."

"Just wait, there are a bevy of delights coming your way," Charlotte said with a snicker. "Swollen ankles."

"Peeing anytime you sneeze, jump, or jar your body in any way," Whitney added.

"Not being able to see your feet."

"Unable to find a comfortable position to sleep in."

"The waddle," Charlotte said, causing them both to laugh out loud.

"Oh, the waddle. I don't miss that," Whitney said, "But I do miss the boobs. Oh, my goodness, I had fabulous breasts when I was pregnant."

"Hers are already great. But, oh, the hemorrhoids."

"I already have those," I said, thankful it was one less thing to look forward to in their list of horrible things to come.

"They'll get worse," Charlotte promised.

"Then there's the emotions. They'll be all over the place. One minute you'll be happy, then angry, then crying..."

"*Jesus*," Margo said, her face full of horror. "Sign me up for *none* of that!"

"Me either," I muttered, feeling less excited than I had when I arrived.

"Sorry, Summer," Whitney said, reaching her hand out toward me. "I promise, it's all worth it. There are not-fun aspects about pregnancy, sure, but the good far outweighs the bad. Like the first time you feel that little flutter in your belly."

"Or when you can see the foot pressing against the side of your stomach and actually see the outline of it," Charlotte said with a knowing smile.

"When you can feel the baby react to the sound of your voice, and Noah's."

"And have we mentioned the boobs? They're going to be magnificent. You'll need a whole new wardrobe just to showcase the girls," Charlotte joked.

"A new wardrobe sounds nice," I agreed. "And Noah does love my breasts."

"He's going to lose his mind," Whitney promised.

Margo looked at all of us and shook her head. "Nope, not worth it."

I grinned at her and said, "Oh, but my little one is going to adore Auntie Margo."

"And I'll spoil the little bugger. But there's no way *this* temple is *ever* going through all of *that*."

"Never say never," Whit warned.

"I just did."

"I never thought I'd have kids either, but then I got married and Nigel said we had to carry on his family name. Of course, then I had Sky, which pissed him off. But now I couldn't imagine my life without her. She's the best."

"He was angry you had a girl instead of a boy?" I asked, unable to fathom it.

Charlotte shrugged and said, "Yeah. He said a girl was of no use to him."

"Wow, what a prick," Margo said with a scowl.

"He really is," Charlotte agreed. "We will be much better off without him."

"Yes, and you have us here for you if you need anything," Whitney said, reassuringly.

"And she doesn't just mean her and Luca and your family, but us, the *Jilted Wives Club*," I told her. "We're your family now, too."

"Damn straight," Margo said, raising her glass once more, but this time saying, "To the *Jilted Wives Club* and to the assholes who didn't know enough to treat us like the queens we are ... good riddance."

"Good riddance," we all cheered.

36

NOAH

"Man, are you serious? You're gonna be a daddy and you're going to ask Summer to marry you?" Trent exclaimed, *right in the middle of my lecture hall.*

It sounded like half the class groaned out loud, causing me to look out over at them with a frown, while Trent chuckled.

"Hey, did you not notice I was whispering?" I chided. "They're taking a test."

"Sorry, couldn't help myself. But the girls in this class will be crying themselves to sleep tonight now that they know sexy professor is off the market."

"*Stop*," I told him in a hushed tone.

"Simply stating facts," Trent teased. "I can't believe this, Noah. It hasn't been that long since we spoke. How could so much have changed so quickly?"

I glanced at him, completely baffled. "You tell me?" I said with a sharp laugh. "I thought Summer had the flu, but no, and everything has spiraled since then."

"But you're definitely going to ask her to marry you?"

"Yeah, I was actually thinking along those lines before I knew she was pregnant, but now, I'm positive. This is what I've been waiting for, Trent. A family. And Summer is more perfect than I'd ever imagined. I have no idea how I got so lucky."

"And to think, none of this would have happened without me."

"How so?" I asked, cocking an eyebrow at his self-satisfied expression.

"I'm the one who dared you to join the True Love app, which you never deleted. Summer saw you on the app and liked you, but made a mistake and deleted you, ergo, Margo saw you at the bar and came over to give you Summer's number. *You're welcome*."

"But I didn't call her. She saw me in the grocery store and came over."

"Still wouldn't have happened without the app."

I shrugged, conceding his point.

"So, how are you going to do it?" he asked.

"What?"

"Propose?"

"Uh, I don't know ... get a ring. Get down on one knee. The usual," I replied.

"My god, it would be cute if you weren't so freaking clueless."

"What do you mean?"

"No one just gets down on one knee anymore. There has to be this whole big thing," he said, throwing his hands up as if he were exasperated. *With me*. "First you have to plan it all out. Then you have to let one of her friends know, so she can make sure Summer has her nails done and her hair done and is dressed up nicely for pictures. Because there have to be pictures. Some women even want you to have a photographer on hand, hiding in the shadows to snap candids of the proposal."

"Are you being serious right now?"

"Totally, Mr. Mason," one of the girls from my class called out. "You can't just spring it on her when she has bed head or something. And the nails are a must, because she's going to want to show off the rock you got her. You are getting a rock, right? The ring is, like, the most important thing."

I looked out over the students and noticed all of the females were nodding in agreement.

"What else do I need to know?" I asked, feeling a pit in my stomach.

"Location is key," Ms. Sinclair added with a look of resignation. "Lots of people like the beach."

"The beach?" We were at least three hours from any beaches.

"Yeah, but parks work, too. Or, like, the zoo, anywhere that has meaning for the two of you. A place that you went, or somewhere you always said you'd go, but haven't. Destination proposals are cool, too."

Holy crap. Destination proposals? They've all lost their minds.

"What happened to good, old-fashioned romance? Spontaneity?" I asked.

"Oh, romance is a must, but so is the other stuff," another young lady said.

I glanced at Trent, who was nodding in agreement.

"Okay, well, it looks like I have a lot to figure out. Now, everyone, back to work."

My mind was reeling for the rest of the day.

I'd already gotten the ring, one I thought was perfectly Summer and I hoped she'd love. But it looked like I had some planning to do. Apparently, I couldn't just take her to dinner and propose like some low-level punk. I'd have to put some thought and effort into it.

And hire a photographer.

I wondered if it had to be a professional, or if I could simply ask my brother Charles to follow us around.

He always took pretty good pictures.

I sighed as I drove home, unsure of what my next move should be. Figuring a woman's point of view might help, I gave my sister-in-law, Jamilla, a call.

"What's up, sexy prof," she said in greeting.

"Oh, have we shortened it now?" I asked wryly.

"Yeah, I was just trying it out," she said with a laugh. "I think I like it."

"I need your help," I said, getting straight to it.

"Uh-oh, women problems?"

"No, everything's great. It's just ...come to my attention ... that in today's popular culture, marriage proposals are a *really* big deal."

"Ahhh, yes. Is my big bro looking to pop the question?"

"I am."

"Does Charles know?"

"No, I haven't told him yet."

"Ha, yes. I am going to gloat so hard."

"Jamilla ... can you help? I've been told she needs to have her nails done and think she's going somewhere where she would want to be dressed up. Also, there should be paparazzi on hand."

Jamilla chuckled, which made me smile.

"My big question is, how? Where? I've never been known for grand gestures. I'm kind of at a loss here."

"Okay, you've called the right person. Here's what you're going to do..."

37
SUMMER

"I'm so glad we're doing this," I told Whitney and Margo as we walked through the city center.

We'd had a fantastic *Women's Day Out*. We'd gotten manis and pedis, went shopping for new lingerie for my already blossoming bosom, gotten blowouts, and I was currently wearing a fabulous new dress Margo had insisted on buying for me.

It was a really fun day of self-care and I'd been surprised how much I'd really needed it.

Especially that pedicure. *Lord,* having my feet rubbed had felt amazing.

Our last stop was going to be dinner downtown, in this cute Italian place with outdoor seating right in the city center.

"Do you mind if we stop here for a minute?" Whitney said, pointing to a bench right in front of the fountain. "I think I have something in my shoe."

"Sure," I said, but Margo already had me by the elbow and was leading me to the bench.

We all sat down, and I was about to say something, when suddenly music began to play and Chris Young's *Who I Am With You* began blaring through the area. My jaw dropped when the seemingly random people grouped together and began to dance.

"*Oh my gosh*, you guys, it's a flash mob!" I yelled to Whit and Margo over the song.

When I caught the look on Margo's face, my head swung back in time to see Noah come front and center of the group and join into the line dance.

His face was bright red, but his smile took up his whole face and his eyes were rapt on me as he moved.

Whitney gave me a little shove, so I got up off of the bench and moved in closer.

The words of the song began to register, and my hands flew to my mouth.

Is this really happening?

I laughed, I cried, and eventually started to move along to the music as I enjoyed the performance Noah had planned for me.

When the song died down, everyone started moving around as if the flash mob had never happened, and Noah got down on one knee in front of me.

He opened the ring box to reveal a cushion-cut engagement ring with a yellow diamond shining brightly in the center.

"*Oh, Noah*," I cried as my entire body began to involuntarily shake.

"Summer," he began, his tone gruff. "From the moment I saw you, I knew you were too good for me. For some reason, you wanted to date me anyway. Over the last few months, I've learned what a kind, smart, honest, amazing woman you are. You're undeniably gorgeous on the outside, but that's no match for the beauty of your heart. I can't believe you not only deemed to love me, but you're giving me the family I've always dreamed of."

Noah paused and I could tell he was trying to fight against the emotion that was welling up inside of him.

"It would be the great honor of my life, if you would agree to be my wife."

I knelt down with him and cupped his cheeks with my hands.

"Yes, I would love to marry you."

He slid the ring on my finger, and we kissed to the sound of Margo and Whitney cheering behind us.

Noah stood and helped me to my feet, and I threw myself into his arms with a joyful laugh.

"I can't believe you did all that!"

Noah grinned at me and said, "I had help from some friends. Did you like it?"

"It's the best thing that has ever happened to me. I've never been so surprised."

"Good," he said, giving me another quick kiss. "And it's just getting started."

"What do you mean?" I asked as he set me back on the ground.

"That dinner we have planned," Whitney said as she and Margo joined us.

"Yeah?"

"It's your engagement party!" Margo shouted gleefully.

"Really?" I asked, my eyes getting watery again. "You planned a party, too?"

"Like I said, I had help," Noah replied. "But, yes, everyone is waiting for us right now. In fact..."

He pointed toward the restaurant, where a crowd of our family and friends stood in the outside dining area. Apparently, they had all watched the proposal as well.

I laced my fingers through his and we moved down the walkway to join our engagement party. We were met with cheers and congratulations, then we all moved inside, since Noah had reserved the entire restaurant for our party.

We were immediately pulled aside by Noah's parents, who were obviously thrilled by the engagement and couldn't believe Noah had been in a flash mob.

"You danced in front of all those people. You were so brave."

"Thanks, Mom," Noah said sheepishly.

"I have *never* been so surprised in my life," I said happily, sliding my arm around his waist.

"Me neither," his father agreed.

We moved around the room, speaking with Jamilla and Charles and Trent and Cam, before moving to say hi to Luca and Whitney's kids, Stella and Silas. Then we briefly greeted Helen and my mom, who were standing off to the side, kind of on their own.

I was touched Noah had asked her, even though he'd probably had an internal debate over it ... I know I would have. But knowing Helen, she'd keep my mom in check and on her best behavior. And as long as she didn't make a fuss, she'd be invited to the wedding as well.

But I'd wait to tell her about the baby. I didn't want to chance her doing or saying something to sour my happy day.

It was a lovely, festive, and extremely thoughtful occasion. And when, at the end of the night, Noah handed me a thumb drive with pictures of all of it, I was absolutely floored.

"You really did think of everything."

"Like I said..."

"You had help, I know," I replied, leaning in to hug him tightly. "But you're the one who was thoughtful enough to make it all happen. You truly are a gift, Noah. I've never been so happy. I love you."

"I love you, too. And you deserve to have a day dedicated to sweeping you off your feet."

EPILOGUE
SUMMER

"You were right, I do miss being able to see my feet," I said as I inelegantly plopped into my chair.

I'd officially moved into Noah's house ... *our house* ... a few weeks ago and we'd finally finished unpacking and finding a place for all of our things to coexist.

"How are you feeling otherwise?" Whitney asked, sitting on the sofa across from me.

"Pretty great, actually. Like super horny."

Whit chuckled and said, "One of the perks I'm sure Noah is enjoying."

"I've heard no complaints."

"Are you excited?" she asked. I'd had the doctor tell her the sex of the baby and she'd had a gender reveal cake made for us. He didn't know anything about it, and I'd decided to keep it something special between us, rather than having a party for it.

We could tell everyone after we'd had the chance to celebrate ourselves.

"I am. Are you sure you don't want to give me a little hint?" I asked.

"No way, my lips are sealed ... I promised."

I'd made her vow not to tell me, no matter how much I begged.

Just then, we heard Noah's keys jingle as he opened the front door and came inside.

"Hello, hello, Daddy's home," he called out, causing me to fall into a fit of giggles.

When he walked into the room and saw Whitney grinning at him from the couch, Noah's face turned bright red.

"Oh, uh, hey, I didn't realize we had company."

"Not company, just me, *Daddy*," Whitney joked as she stood up and moved to give him a quick hug. "In fact, I'll leave you guys too it. Have fun and call me later, Summer."

"Thanks again, Whit."

"Anytime, babe."

"Well, that was embarrassing," Noah said as I crossed to give him a kiss.

"Don't worry about it," I assured him. "Come on, I've got a surprise for you."

"Is it bigger than the, *I think I'm pregnant* thing, because I'm not sure I can take anything else."

"Ha ha," I said dryly as I pulled him into the kitchen.

"Dessert for dinner?" he asked when he saw the cake sitting on the counter.

"It's a special cake," I informed him slyly.

"How so?"

"Well, when we cut into it, it will reveal if we're having a boy or a girl."

"Really?" Noah asked gleefully.

He grabbed the chef's knife out of the butcher block and held it out. "Shall we?" he asked.

I nodded and placed my hand over his on the handle of the knife, and then together we cut a large slice.

"Ready?" I asked, my voice shaking with excitement.

He nodded and we slid the knife under the slice and eased it out.

The cake was blue.

"A boy?" Noah breathed.

"It's a boy!" I shouted, letting the knife go at the same time he did.

As it clattered to the counter I stared at the cake.

"I really thought it was a girl."

"Are you disappointed?" he asked.

I looked up at him with a happy smile and tears streaming down my face. "Not at all. I can't wait to meet him. I already love him so much."

"I know," Noah said, pulling me in close. "I can't wait to teach him to swim, and to read, and all about dangling participles."

"You're such a delicious weirdo," I told him as I laughed, so happy it was hard to believe I'd ever been anything else.

"I'm your delicious weirdo," he said, leaning down to nuzzle my nose with his.

"Yes, you are," I agreed, looking up at him with all the love in my heart. "Forever mine."

WHAT'S NEXT?

Want more of *The Jilted Wives Club*? Keep reading for Chapter One of Work Wife - Preorder Now!

WORK WIFE

Chapter 1 - Margo

"I STILL LIVE WITH MY MOTHER, BUT IT'S REALLY FOR HER sake. She doesn't want to be alone, and she likes having me there to take care of. I'm kinda in between jobs right now, but I think I'd like to be an actor. There just aren't really any acting jobs here in the city. Anyway..." He paused to cough in rapid succession. "Don't worry, it's just a sore throat and cough. No big deal."

Somebody shoot me.

I swear to God, Summer is going to owe me big time for this.

I backed further away in my seat to try and avoid his germs.

The speed dating event Summer had asked me to come to in her place was just kicking off, and this guy was my first "date". He'd been talking about himself from the moment he sat down and hadn't asked me one thing about myself.

I seriously hoped our five minutes was almost up.

"Okay, fellas, switch," the moderator said.

All of the men stood up and walked to the next table, while

all of the women stayed put.

"Hi, I'm Margo," I said to the tall drink of water who sat across from me.

"I'm Philip."

"Where are you from Philip?" I asked, noting his accent.

"I actually live in France. I am only here for the weekend on business. I saw the app was hosting this event and thought I'd check it out."

Okay, so this dude's definitely just looking to hookup.

Once the moderator told them to switch again, I crossed off the first guy's name and put a check mark next to the second because... who knew. He may be the best bet I had for the night.

And on the party went.

Some of the guys were okay. But if they mentioned marriage or kids, I crossed them off my list. There was no way I was looking to get bogged down with a guy in search of a serious commitment.

I was doodling on my paper when the next guy sat down and when I looked up to see longish black hair framing a tanned, lean face with bright blue eyes, my spidey senses started to tingle.

I instinctively held out my hand and said huskily, "Margo."

His answering grin was slightly lopsided, and his hand was rough with callouses. The hands of a man who worked for a living, not like the guys in my office, or my ex.

All of this worked for me. *A lot.*

"Aiden," he replied in a deep voice that sent shivers down my spine.

Wow. Aiden was definitely a winner.

"Have you been to one of these before, Aiden?" I asked, praying he said no. I'd hate to learn he was a regular on the dating app scene.

"No, this is my first time. You?" he asked.

"Same," I replied, then leaned in close and admitted, "Actually, I don't even belong to the app, I'm here doing a favor for a friend."

"Ah," Aiden said, that deep voice seeming to rumble through me. "You are single though, right? Or are you simply here for fun?"

"Single. But also, here for fun," I teased, leaning in a smidge closer.

I could smell his cologne, which was dark and woodsy, and feel the heat coming off of his body.

"I see," he said, smoothly.

"Do you? Because I'd love to get your number," I said, going out on a limb and not caring in the slightest.

He was the most interesting man I'd met recently. And not just tonight, but in the last few months. Hell, he may have been the first guy to get this kind of instant reaction out of me in years.

"How about you talk to me after?" Aiden suggested.

The deal was we would have five minutes with each guy and then after there'd be a kind of social hour, where you could talk more in depth with the people who caught your eye.

"I'll do that," I promised, just as the announcer said to move.

I watched Aiden get up, enjoying the way he seemed to unfold himself from the chair. He was really tall, which appealed to me, since I was five feet ten inches myself.

When a new guy sat down, I sighed with regret and turned my attention to him.

Great. He looks like he could be my nephew.

The night went on, painstakingly slow, until finally, the last guy left my table, and I was free to move about the room.

After going to the bar to get a drink, I turned slowly and surveyed the room.

There...

Aiden was talking to a petite blonde by the snack bar, but I paid no attention to her. I stood to my full height, brushed my long black hair off my shoulders and sauntered over to where he was standing.

My movement caught his attention and his gaze looked me over as I sidled up beside him.

He gave me that lopsided grin, turned his attention back to the blonde, and said, "It was great meeting you, too, Jess."

She gave him a big smile, which dimmed a little when she looked at me, and then turned her hair whipping around, and flounced to the bar.

"Hey there," I said, once she was gone.

"Hey. Did you enjoy your first time speed dating?"

I gave a half shrug and said, "I consider my favor complete. How about you?"

"I met some nice people."

"Yeah?" I asked. "Anyone of note?"

"I'm not sure there was anyone I really had anything in common with."

"How about chemistry?"

"There may have been one person I felt a hint of a spark with," he teased.

I lengthened my spine and pushed back my shoulders to showcase my bosom. My breasts were small, but I knew how to work 'em.

Aiden's gaze was knowing, but rather than take the bait, he simply smiled. When his tongue darted out to wet his lips, I felt a little lightheaded.

"What do you say we get out of here?" I said, never one to shy away from what I wanted.

"That's quite an offer," Aiden said. "But I'm afraid I'm going to have to take a rain check. I've got a busy morning tomorrow."

Disappointment filled me at his words, but I wasn't one to beg, so I looked him straight in the eye and said, "Your loss," and walked out the front door.

THE JILTED WIVES CLUB PLAYLIST

I Would've Loved You by Jake Hoot & Kelly Clarkson
I Hope by Gabby Barrett
Before He Cheats by Carrie Underwood
Say Something by A Great Big World featuring Christina Aguilera
Torn by Natalie Imbruglia
Jar of Hearts by Christina Perri
Someone You Loved by Lewis Capaldi
I Can't Make You Love Me by Bonnie Raitt
Lose You to Love Me by Selena Gomez
So What by P!nk

Return to Love by Andrea Bocelli featuring Ellie Goulding
Who I Am With You by Chris Young

ACKNOWLEDGMENTS

To my kids, always! I'm so proud of you and grateful for your support.

To my mom, Ann, and to Raine, for Alpha reading and loving Noah as much as I do.

To Allie, my cover designer. I really love the cover concept for this series. You're amazing!

To Kristina, my editor, thanks for all you've done over the years and for your constant support.

To Ali, Jennifer, Lyn, and Jeanne, for Beta reading. I appreciate your support and willingness to read my words!

To Jessica and Inkslinger PR, thanks for all your hard work and dedication to helping get the word out!

To my ARC Team, I always appreciate your feedback and the way you feel for the characters.

ABOUT THE AUTHOR

Bethany Lopez is a USA Today Bestselling author of more than thirty books and has been published since 2011. She's a lover of all things romance, which she incorporates into the books she writes, no matter the genre.

When she isn't reading or writing, she loves spending time with family and traveling whenever possible.

Bethany can usually be found with a cup of coffee or glass of wine at hand, and will never turn down a cupcake!

To learn more about upcoming events and releases, sign up for my newsletter.

www.bethanylopezauthor.com
bethanylopezauthor@gmail.com

Follow her at https://www.bookbub.com/authors/bethany-lopez *to get an alert whenever she has a new release, preorder, or discount!*

ALSO BY BETHANY LOPEZ

Contemporary Romance:

The Jilted Wives Club Trilogy

Starter Wife

Trophy Wife - Preorder Now

Work Wife - Preorder Now

Backup Wife - Preorder Now

Mason Creek Series

Perfect Summer

A Time for Love Series

Prequel - 1 Night - FREE

8 Weeks - FREE

21 Days

42 Hours

15 Minutes

10 Years

3 Seconds

7 Months

For Eternity - Novella

Night & Day - Novella

Time for Love Series Box Set

Time to Risk

The Lewis Cousins Series

Too Tempting - FREE

Too Complicated

Too Distracting

Too Enchanting

Too Dangerous

The Lewis Cousins Box Set

Summer Love Anthology featuring Too Enticing

Three Sisters Catering Trilogy

A Pinch of Salt

A Touch of Cinnamon

A Splash of Vanilla

Three Sisters Catering Trilogy Box Set

Frat House Confessions

Frat House Confessions: Ridge

Frat House Confessions: Wes

Frat House Confessions: Brody

Frat House Confessions 1 - 3 Box Set

Frat House Confessions: Crush - Coming Soon

Romantic Comedy/Suspense:

Delilah Horton Series

Always Room for Cupcakes - FREE

Cupcake Overload

Lei'd with Cupcakes

Cupcake Explosion

Cupcakes & Macaroons - Honeymoon Short - FREE

Lei'd in Paradise - Novella (Carmen & Bran)

Crazy for Cupcakes - Coming Soon

Women's Fiction:

More than Exist

Unwoven Ties

Short Stories/Novellas:

Contemporary:

Christmas Come Early

Harem Night

Reunion Fling

An Inconvenient Dare

Snowflakes & Country Songs

Fool for You - FREE

Desert Alpha (Lady Boss Press Navy SEAL Novella)

Fantasy:

Leap of Faith

Beau and the Beastess

Cookbook:

Love & Recipes

Love & Cupcakes

Children's:

Katie and the North Star

Young Adult:

Stories about Melissa – series

Ta Ta for Now!

xoxoxo

Ciao

TTYL

Stories About Melissa Books 1 - 4

With Love

Adios

Young Adult Fantasy:

Nissa: a contemporary fairy tale

New Adult:

Friends & Lovers Trilogy

Make it Last

I Choose You

Trust in Me

Indelible